RUBY FERGUSON

Jill's Pony Trek

**COVER AND TEXT
ILLUSTRATIONS
BY CANEY**

ARMADA
PAPERBACKS
for Boys & Girls

How We Thought About It

BEING seventeen has its points, but there are moments when one feels very dim about such things as being too old for the pony classes, and having to take life seriously and think about a career, and one's mind hies back to the gorgeous experiences of one's carefree youth when it was ponies, ponies all the way.

I began to wonder if there were any of those experiences which I hadn't yet related to my gloating readers, and if so, would it do me any good to recall them now, or should I just howl with anguish at the thought of having exchanged the riding stick for the sordid ball-point pen?

"You never told them about that pony trek," said my friend Ann Derry.

"What pony trek?" I said without much interest.

"Miss Crombie's pony trek."

I sat up from where I had been lying on the rug in front of the fire, letting the new puppy bite my hair, and said firmly, "It wasn't Miss Crombie's pony trek. Miss Crombie never even went. It started with that Mrs. Folds who had a brother who had a riding school. I don't remember how Miss Crombie came into it at all."

"But she jolly well did, you know."

"Gosh!" I said. "So she did. I'd forgotten about Miss Crombie since she went to live at Bournemouth or somewhere."

Ann said I must be slipping if I went on forgetting people and things like that, and I ought to take a memory course, and I said there was nothing wrong with my memory, and soon we were having an absolute ding-dong, just like old times, and Mummy came in and said anybody listening to us would think it was break-time in the kindergarten, and could we make less row as she was just about to start a new book and couldn't get the first sentence going.

Ann said, "Jill's going to start a new book too, and she doesn't even know what it's going to be about."

But I suddenly realised that I did know what it was going to be about, and I even remembered that it all began one morning at school, in geometry of all things.

We had a new geometry mistress that term called Miss Pyck. I expect she had put the "y" in herself to make it more interesting, but of course we called her The Shovel, except for the sixth form who tried to be subtle and called her Choosey.

So I was sitting at my desk in a beautiful golden dream when she suddenly asked me, "Jill, could you bear to tell us what kind of an angle we shall have in segment A of Circle B?"

I didn't know what she was talking about as I had been out on Cloud Seven for several minutes, and hadn't even noticed any Circle A, so I just gaped and she said, "I thought so. Take an order mark for inattention."

6

What I had been thinking about was a library book which Ann and I had just read called *Pony Trekking in Ecuador*. A smashing book. Neither of us had much idea where Ecuador was, except that it must be a world away from our own sordid orbit, but it sounded a pretty good place. One thing about Ecuador was that it didn't seem to be cluttered up with any gruesome ideas about end of term exams, or tidying up as you go, or order marks, or cleaning the hens on Saturday mornings. In Ecuador you hurled a few carefree nothings into saddle-bags whenever you felt like it, and got on a pony and set out for romance and adventure.

I felt bitter about that order mark. Order marks went down on your report, and I already had five, and there was still another week of term, and Mummy would be livid as they were all for the same thing, in-attention, which I felt wasn't a fair description as all I was doing was dreaming of nobler things than what-ever it was I was supposed to be inattentive about, which makes sense to me if it doesn't to you.

When we went out for break I told Ann what I thought about this, and she said, "Blow The Shovel! Can't you think about something else and look as if you were listening to her? I can. And by the way, would you like to sell flags on Saturday for the Horse Protection Society, because Captain Todd is looking for people and I said I would."

"I don't mind," I said without enthusiasm, "but I'm not much good at it. The people I catch always put pennies in, and the people other people catch put half-crowns in, and my cousin Cecilia got eight pounds in her tin for the Spastics and I only got twenty-one and four, and mine was all in pennies and she had three pound notes and heaps of silver, and then she said I hadn't tried. Tried!" I gave a sort of hollow, tragic laugh.

"Gosh, you are in a mood," said Ann.

"If only I lived in Ecuador," I said, kicking the railing outside the gym. "Always pony trekking, never selling flags or keeping hens. Hens!"

Mummy's hen-interests were a sore point with me, because though profitable they are otherwise almost a dead loss since they are not creatures you can get fond of, and would not if you could since you later eat them. I often wished that Mummy could have found herself a more glamorous side-line which did not involve my toiling among feathered morons with no more reward than an occasional chicken dinner. My only consolation was dreaming day-dreams in which the hens became so profitable that Mummy bought a farm for them with lots of outbuildings in which I could gradually accumulate a lot of ponies and start a riding school, which in its turn would become so successful that it would eliminate the hens for which the farm was originally started.

"I'm sick of hearing about Ecuador," said Ann. "I wish you'd snap out of it."

I didn't think this exactly sympathetic, and told her so, and added that it was a good thing her flag day was for something horsy as otherwise I wouldn't have touched it with a barge pole, and she said did I mean that if it had been orphans I wouldn't have done it?—and I said that's what I did mean, and she said she never heard of anything so mean and grudging, and then the bell rang and we stalked into school.

At home I had a quiet sort of evening, reading, and Mummy said, "Isn't Ann coming round?"

I dipped rather dolefully into a packet of liquorice allsorts to find the ones I like best, which are like little black swiss rolls, and said, "No. We had a slight row," and Mummy said, "Don't be childish, what was it about?" and I said, "Oh, Ecuador and orphans and things," and it sounded so silly that I started giggling.

So Saturday came round, and Ann and I found ourselves outside the Supermarket with our trays of flags. Everybody was shopping and we pounced on them when they had their purses in their hands, and did very well. When our tins got too heavy we took them to be counted. I had got twenty-five shillings, nearly all in copper—as usual, and Ann had got three pounds fifteen with heaps of half-crowns. Fate again!

Then Captain Todd said, what about calling at a few houses? I thought this was a good idea, but Ann wanted to go back to the Supermarket, so we parted and I set off towards Poplar Road, making up my mind as I went that I'd get more money than Ann this time or die.

Unfortunately, at the first house, a woman came to the door and said she had already bought a flag from me at the Supermarket, and didn't I remember? It wasn't a very good start.

The next house was Miss Crombie's, and it was whimsically called *Dovecotes* though there wasn't a cote much less a dove in sight. I can never understand why people do that kind of thing. Perhaps they think that if they call their house *Laburnum Bower* it may miraculously develop one during the night, but myself I like plain, true sort of names like *Pool Cottage*, which is ours, or *Hill House*, or just *Lane End* if that is where your house is situated.

Ann once said she didn't entirely agree with me about this, or her house would be called *Bus Terminus Villa* which was where it happened to be, and I said

9

I would rather that than *Corrivale* which it is actually called and which doesn't mean a thing.

Anyway, there I was at Miss Crombie's door, pressing the bell button, which was one of those that is yellow in the daylight and at night lights up orange all by itself, and I wondered how it did it, and wished we had one.

The Day I Didn't Shine

MISS CROMBIE opened the door. All I knew about her was that somebody had told me she was always writing letters to *Horse and Hound* and some times got one in. I once wrote a letter to *Horse and Hound* myself, and though I thought it was the last word it never got printed, so Miss Crombie's letters must have been stiff with impressive horsy know-how.

Miss Crombie looked at my tray and said, "Oh—flags," as if she'd been expecting Father Christmas. But when I told her the noble object was the protection of horses she brightened up and said I was to come in and go into the sitting-room and she'd find her purse.

The sitting-room was quite interesting. It looked as if the contents of a much bigger room had been tipped into it regardless of fit. There were so many chairs and tables and book-stands and newspaper racks and cabinets that you could hardly see the carpet, and every little table had a table lamp and needlework and books and small boxes on it, and I thought, what a gorgeous room for a blindfold obstacle race—crash crash, crash!

11

All over the place were photographs of a woman on a smashing grey mare, and after a few amazed moments of thinking what a lot of sisters and cousins Miss Crombie must have, I realised that they were all Miss Crombie herself. It must give you a weird feeling to live surrounded by photographs of yourself, and I'm sure Mummy wouldn't let me even if I wanted to, but Miss Crombie couldn't have felt the same about it.

At this point in my reflections I knocked over a small table and a sheet of writing-paper went flying. As I picked it up I couldn't help seeing what was written on it:

To the Editor of Horse and Hound.
Dear Sir,
    The future of British riding lies in the young entry. I have always——

Well! I thought. That's not so marvellous. I knew that myself, and I should have thought the editor did.

Just then Miss Crombie came in, and proceeded to stuff a pound note into my collecting box.

"Oh, thank you most frightfully!" I gasped. "This is jolly well going to shove my total up."

I pushed a flag into her fuzzy brown cardigan.

"How old are you, my child?" she asked.

"Fourteen."

"And what led you to embark upon this noble task?"

For a minute I didn't know what she was talking about, and then I realised that I was supposed to be noble because I was selling flags, so one thing led to another, and in about ten minutes Miss Crombie and I were sitting cosily over a cup of cocoa, and I found myself telling her my horsy history, and all about my

12

ponies Black Boy and Rapide, and something of my adventures in show ring and field.

I suddenly realised that I was doing what Mummy says I should never do, yakking on about myself, so I switched and said, "All those photographs are of you, aren't they?"

"You noticed?" she said, looking a bit droopy. "Ah. Everything passes, everything dies."

I took it that the grey mare was dead and said, "What a frightful shame," but it turned out that it wasn't dead at all but had been passed on to Miss Crombie's niece who was madly winning everything on it in Shropshire.

"As for me," she said with wistful pride, "I was born in the saddle."

I gaped like a fish. I had often come across this exciting phrase but never from anybody who actually claimed it.

"But the glorious days are over," she went on dreamily. "Two severe tosses in the hunting field put me on my back for months, and soon I learned that I should never ride again. As I could never bring myself just to amble about on a pony, I—who so to speak had scaled the heights—closed the stable door for ever on my hopes and joys."

I went on gaping. She wasn't kidding, she was dead serious, and I wouldn't have believed that anybody could actually talk so much like a book which Ann and I had had out of the library, called *Lady Di and her Arab*.

This book had struck us as not being like any pony book we had read before, and for a bit we had had Lady Di on the brain.

"Come," said Miss Crombie, "you mustn't take my tragedy too much to heart."

13

"I wasn't," I said, and then thinking that this sounded rather rude, I rushed on, "I was just wondering if you'd ever read a book called *Lady Di and her Arab*? Because Lady Di was like you, she broke every single bone taking frightful tosses, and she lay sobbing in a darkened room thinking all was over, and her gorgeous Arab sold to some unworthy stranger, until she realised it was not the end and she could still find joy in helping others."

"So what did she do?" asked Miss Crombie.

I said I thought the end was a bit tame really, because Lady Di just took an interest in the local pony club, and the last thing the children saw before they went into the ring was her sweet smiling face and it helped them over the jumps—(though how I don't know, because they ought to have been thinking about their aids and not people's sweet smiling faces which would have put me, for one, right off)—but anyway it was only a story.

Miss Crombie said she thought it was a marvellous story, and she brought out some mint imperials and we had a few, and she said she, like Lady Di, was only interested now in the young entry, and in fact she was just writing to the editor of *Horse and Hound* to suggest that older riders should spend more time encouraging the young and less time sitting round the clubroom fire, and when I finally said I would have to go she added, "Do let me know next time you're going to ride in any event, and I'll come round and watch you. I shall be able to see my youth reflected in you."

I said it was very kind of her, and hurried away, because I was just on the verge of giggling, which would have been extremely rude. I managed to sell a few more flags, and went back to join Ann, and to tell her about Miss Crombie.

"Gosh," I said, "she's exactly like Lady Di. You wouldn't believe it possible unless you saw her."

A few days later Ann shoved a schedule under my nose, and said, "Here's a chance for your Miss Crombie to renew her youth in you, or whatever she said. Pony gymkhana at Lowis Hill on Saturday week, all the usual events. They've got quite a decent pony club at Lowis Hill and they're all very keen."

"I hope they're not too marvellous," I said. "If I get outclassed by them, Miss Crombie won't see anything reflected anywhere—except mud—and neither will I."

"Don't be silly," Ann said. "She'd just be sorry for you."

"I don't want anybody to be sorry for me!" I yelled. "I want to win!"

"Oh, you horrible pot hunter," said Ann.

"No I'm not, and you know what I mean," I said. "I suppose you're going to enter too?"

Ann said she might as well. It would be nice if we could get Miss Crombie interested in the local entry, and if she proved to be rich as well as horsy she might be persuaded to put up the money for a really good one-day event and give a few cups and so on, and I saw the point of this, though I wasn't as confident as Ann that the sight of our riding would inspire Miss Crombie all that much.

Ann said the thing was to look keen, and if necessary to be good losers, because that might appeal to a person like Miss Crombie more than if we actually won, and make her want to encourage us, and I said, "Oh, stop it."

Eventually I was persuaded to go round to Miss Crombie's to tell her about the gymkhana at Lowis Hill, and she was absolutely thrilled.

"I'll tell you what," she said. "I'll be your pony

girl. Now don't say 'Don't bother,' because I shall love to do all the work."

I thought, Oh, Crumbs!

In the first place, I'd never in my life had anybody to act as groom or pony girl for me, and I couldn't see myself lolling in the refreshment tent with such squares as Susan Pyke while somebody else groomed my pony and kept the flies off him. Again, if Miss Crombie had been young I wouldn't have minded so much, but she must have been about forty and it seemed awful to make anybody so old toil for you while you lounged in sordid indolence.

So I just said, "Thank you very much," and looked awkward, and got away as soon as I could.

"You let her do it," said Ann. "She'll enjoy it. I mean, think of Lady Di. It would be just her cup of tea."

"I just wonder what she'll wear," I said. "She rather likes frills and bows and things. Do you remember that kid's mother once, with fur bands on her sleeves, and the pony chewed off the fur and was too sick to go in the event? I'd die if that happened."

"It couldn't," said Ann. "If she looks awful we'll manage to lose her."

I felt the last person it would be easy to lose would be Miss Crombie.

"I'm calling for her on Saturday at twelve," I said glumly.

"Well, don't beef about it," Ann said. "You started it. By the way, I hear that Lowis Hill's two best people are out of the gymkhana. One's pony is coughing and the other one has to go to the Isle of Wight with her people. So it gives us a better chance of pulling something off."

I said that I hoped it wouldn't be too much of a

walkover or Miss Crombie wouldn't be at all impressed, and Ann said it couldn't possibly be a walkover as the Lowis Hill standard had always been pretty high, and I said, in that case we'd both be lucky if we picked up a couple of rosettes in the Child's Pony Self-Groomed and Schooled, never mind the riding classes.

How We Met Somebody

WHEN the day came I dressed with a good deal of care as I didn't want to look kiddish. If you are fourteen and rather thin, you are apt to find yourself looking about twelve in your blue shirt and your two-year-old jodhs which are a bit tight and short in the leg, only your mother says they are still wearable. I back-combed my hair a bit, and looked in the looking-glass with a sort of grown-up scowl, and breathed a dark-brown groan, and put on some more lipstick and then scrubbed most of it off as I knew Mummy would make me anyway.

Those of you who have read my previous books will know about our doings at Chatton and about my friends. We were all keen riders, and spent our spare time seeking competitions and all kinds of pony interests, and we had wonderful people to help us, like Mrs. Darcy who ran the riding school, and Mercy Dulbottle's aunt who gave us a field for the Pony Club, and Captain Cholly-Sawcutt who had been a member of the British Show-Jumping Team and was particularly good to me because I had taken on the almost impossible task of teaching his dud but cheerful daughters to ride, and many others. So we were exceptionally lucky, and we were always looking for new things to do and new pony adventures.

So getting ready for a gymkhana was one of the things I had been doing for years, and yet I still got the needle about it, wondering if I was going to look all right and do well.

I deepened my scowl, shoved a grip in my hair to make it stick up more, and went out to get Rapide. My intention had been to ride Black Boy that afternoon, but he had got a slight laceration on the knee (by being silly going through a gate) and Ann, who was more than fussy about injuries, had been telling me the awful things that might happen, to the extent of him going downright lame, so it had to be Rapide, and there he stood in his stall, turning round to make faces at me, and looking extremely well-groomed after all my efforts. I had been at him since eight o'clock, and his sleek shining appearance was a credit.

"Now look," I said to him, "if you play me up to-day I've done with you. Get that?" He gave a slight grin.

I had been putting him through some much-needed jumping practice and he had treated it as one huge lark, looking at each jump with a what-on-earth's this? expression, and then approaching it sideways, throwing his head and swinging his rump. I knew he was doing this on purpose, because he well knew the difference between practice (which bored him) and the real thing (which was a chance to do what he adored doing—showing off) but it wasn't encouraging for me.

"I've told you!" I said, very sinister, as I gave his tail a final brush. He rolled his eyes like a bored film star, and when I ticked him off for that he nuzzled my shoulder. Rapide always understood every word I said to him.

19

Ann arrived, and I told her that Miss Crombie had rung up to say she would go over to Lowis Hill on her bike and meet us there, so we hacked over, and she was waiting for us just inside the field gate, hopping with excitement.

"Everybody's here," she said. "And it's a wonderful day. Sunny, but not too hot. And you both look *beautiful*. And what gorgeous ponies!"

She didn't look at all bad. She had on a sporting kind of tweed skirt and a white shirt and a tie that looked like Roedean First Eleven Hockey 1892, and even if she had crowned one end of her with a red wool pixie cap and the other with a pair of blinding white gym shoes, that could happen to anybody.

"I've staked us out a very pretty claim under the trees," she said. "Over there. I've dumped my canvas bag. Come on, before there's any argument."

She whisked us over to the spot she had found, and all around us other ponies and riders were gathering, and we saw several people we knew and a whole lot of people we didn't know, and there was the usual atmosphere of excitement and jolly fuss and muddle.

"I'll just dust the ponies down," said Miss Crombie, "and give them a flick with the rubber—like that— now don't you two do a *thing*!"

She was evidently set on being Ann's pony girl as well as mine, but it felt funny to stand on one side and do nothing, and I nearly split with laughing when Rapide turned round at me with *such* a face, and practically said aloud, "Who on earth's this?"

Miss Crombie then produced an enormous canvas bag, and from it fished out a whole bunch of carrots and held them out to Rapide, saying, "Here's a present for a good boy."

"Oh, please don't give him anything to eat," I said.

"Oh, how mean!" said Miss Crombie.

"No, Jill isn't," said Ann. "Rapide will take anything, but he doesn't swallow it, he holds it in his mouth and spits it out at the judge in the showing class."

While we were arguing about this, Ann's pony, George, whom nobody was noticing just then, pushed his nose into the canvas bag, hoicked out another bunch of carrots, and before Ann could stop him bolted six.

"That's the limit!" said Ann going red with rage. "Now he'll get colic."

"Oh, no he won't," said Miss Crombie calmly. "I've got a tablet. You see, I come prepared for everything with my nice big bag. What a story this bag could tell if it could talk! Do you know what Captain Llewellyn used to say? He used to say, 'Miss Crombie, Foxhunter and I always feel safe when we see you and your canvas bag."

"I'd much rather you didn't give George anything, *please*," said Ann. "I mean, he's allergic to anything the vet doesn't give him."

I thought that was rather clever, and Miss Crombie said, "Well, if you say not, but——"

"Oh, look," I interrupted, "everybody but us has got their numbers. Come on, we'll take the ponies with us, they're tired of standing."

This gave us a chance to escape, and we went and collected our numbers, 38 and 39, and tied them on.

"Personally," said Ann, "it wouldn't hurt me to give your Miss C. the slip."

"You won't say that when she whangs out a smacking great subscription for the Pony Club," I said. "The thing is to keep her interested. For instance, if we could be first and second in the showing class——"

Without going back to our base, we rode in for the showing class. Something went wrong. For once Ann's pony seemed to have lost that dignified action which so impressed judges, and Rapide for no reason at all got an urge to drop his head and did so several noticeable times.

We were called in third and fourth, which wasn't what we'd expected. Finally, after the inspection, we were changed round—but with each other, not the higher numbers—and Ann got third and I got reserve, and we cantered off feeling less than pleased.

Miss Crombie was waiting for us, and gave us a lot of consolation by saying that even the greatest riders had their off days, but that didn't help much. I had a feeling that this wasn't going to be a lucky day for me, and I was right. Too right.

You know how it is in competitions, there comes a moment every time when you need the luck and you either have it or you don't, and on this day I just didn't. In the jumping class—junior event—everything Rapide tipped fell down, and a lot of things seemed to fall that he hadn't even tipped. I got twelve faults, and I hadn't had twelve faults for years.

Ann won it. Everything that George did came off. He even hit the top of the wall with a clunk you could have heard a mile away, and nothing fell. The triple bar was a brute, and George hates triple bars anyway, but he went at this one as if he hadn't a chance, and soared over it.

Ann looked stunned when she rode out with the red rosette, and the prize which was four pounds.

"Marvellous!" said Miss Crombie. "Absolutely first rate. Really."

"I never saw so much bad luck as Jill had," said

Ann loyally. "Normally she could have done that course with a blindfold pony and a broken leg. It was just frightful luck."

I could see Miss Crombie struggling not to make the gruesome remark, "There's no such thing as bad luck, only bad judgement."

"Come on," I said to Ann. "There's still the senior thing."

We rode in with the under-sixteens, and I was so careful that I held Rapide to a crawl and expected him to do cat jumps every time. Some of these came off, but more didn't. I got eight faults. Ann wasn't placed either. We rode back to Miss Crombie, who by now must have been getting rather hot and bored with us.

"Jill can't go home without winning *something*," she said, in a tone that was meant to cheer. "You'd better have a bash at some of the games, Jill."

I couldn't say, "Let's call it a day," as I felt like saying, so we went along to the paddock where the games were going on. The bending, in which I might have stood a chance as Rapide adored it, was finished, but they had that race where you pick up handkerchiefs from the top of poles, so we went in for that, and George got bumped by another pony and retired, and I finished second and won two tins of Tussington's Tidy Tack Spray.

"Hurray!" cried Miss Crombie, patting me and Rapide as if we'd got a gold cup. "Splendid!"

She certainly could get enthusiastic about nothing. We went and had some tea in the tent, and then set off to hack home, Ann leading on George, then Rapide and me, and finally Miss Crombie on her wobbly bike.

What happened I couldn't tell, but I thought Rapide must have stepped on a stone which turned under him because he suddenly side-stepped, shot forward,

24

and biffed George full in the beam. George bolted and went off with Ann like a rocket, and Miss Crombie yelled, "After her! Quick! Quick! Help!"

"There's no need to," I said. "Ann's perfectly capable of coping. I don't even know what happened."

"I caught Rapide with my front wheel," Miss Crombie confessed nobly.

"He hates having anything behind him," I said, quieting Rapide down. "He's been in a silly mood all day, too."

"But Ann is out of sight," shrieked Miss Crombie. "Aren't you going to do anything?"

"She can't be in a mess," I said, "or we'd have heard crashes and screams by now. Not to worry."

We trudged on, round the next bend, and there sure enough was Ann with George blowing slightly on the grass verge, calm but annoyed.

Ann wasn't alone. She was talking to a very good-looking woman in a white silk shirt and breeches, holding a chestnut mare of the kind I would buy if I was rich beyond the dreams of avarice, as the books say.

"This is Mrs. Folds," said Ann. "She very kindly stopped George."

"It didn't take much doing," said Mrs. Folds. "The pony stopped when he saw me coming, so I got down to see what was the matter."

I hoped we looked all right, but doubted it. One never looks one's best riding back after a gymkhana, hot and dusty.

"We've been at the Lowis Hill gymkhana," I said.

"Good. Any luck?" said Mrs. Folds.

"Ann won the junior jumping."

"It was a fluke," said Ann.

"Oh?" said Mrs. Folds. "I wonder if any of my

25

brother's pupils were there? He has a riding school, you know, at Bat Leas."

I didn't know, I had never heard of Mrs. Fold's brother, but I thought he was jolly lucky to have a riding school. I mean, what can life hold more?

Ann said, "Thanks awfully for stopping. We'd better be getting along now." And Mrs. Folds said, "Oh, don't go yet. Come round to my place and have some ginger beer. I'm looking for people like you, to go on a pony trek.

Who Goes Pony Trekking

"WHO is she?" asked Mummy. "You can't go off on a pony trek with just anybody you meet casually by the roadside."

This remark may ring a bell in the hearts of many of my panting readers. It is the sort of thing that mothers say.

I said, "If I don't go on the pony trek I'll die. It's the only thing I want to do in the world," and Mummy said, "I wish you wouldn't exaggerate so. All I want to know is some more about the whole affair."

"Mrs. Folds has got a super farm," I said, "and her brother has a riding school, and Diana Bush's cousin goes to it. She was awfully nice and you'd have liked her, and she gave us cake and ginger beer, and she had a huge great Jacobean dresser with a secret drawer in it. And it costs three pounds ten."

"Three pounds ten! A Jacobean——"

"No, the pony trek," I said, "and I've still got the three pounds ten I won at Chatton Show, so that's okay. She really was jolly nice, and if you wonder why she's bothering about us, she said that all children who rode at all ought to have a try at riding in the real country, and it's up to her to help them. We've

27

got to learn to cope with things that happen, like weather and mishaps, and sleeping out, and——"

"Ah," said Mummy. "Damp blankets."

I said coldly that Mrs. Folds was obviously the kind of person who wouldn't have a damp blanket within miles of her, and she'd told us that it brought out the best in a person to have to prepare and cook a satisfying meal after a long day's trek, and Mummy said, "That's one sensible idea!" and I said, "Well, there you are, then."

Mummy finally said that if Ann's mother said that Ann could go, I could go too.

This was cunning of her, because Ann's mother is madly fussy about who Ann goes with, and about airing clothes and first-aid and taking precautions, and other things that grown-ups somehow think you never have any sense about.

So our spirits shot up, and then they bumped down again, as at first Ann's mother said that Ann couldn't go, because there obviously wouldn't be anywhere to dry your wet clothes, and we thought that was the end of it. And then Ann's mother met Mrs. Folds, and it suddenly turned out that they had been at school together—if you can imagine anything so historical—and everything was all right, in fact Ann's mother got so keen on the idea of the pony trek that you would think she had invented it.

That being so, Mummy of course said that I could go, and I was so excited that I ran wildly round and round the orchard with the ponies chasing after me, instead of me chasing after them.

I should think that everybody who is even remotely human must have dreamed about going on a pony trek. My imagination started working overtime, picturing a string of ponies and riders winding its way

28

through a lush valley in the pearly dawn, or the golden noon, or even under the moonlight, with unknown worlds of excitement and adventure ahead, and new thrilling things happening every minute.

I was thinking, of course, of book-like adventures, like discovering a crumbling fane in a forest with buried treasure in the crypt, or saving somebody's life who turned out to be famous, or getting mixed up with some spies and frustrating their evil plans and being given a medal by one's grateful country. (Not the sort of adventures which usually happen to me, and end up with a limping pony and having to stagger five miles home with your arms full of sopping tack.)

A girl I know called Angela Delacourt once went out of her way to put some lost riders on the right track and this started a friendship, and they turned out to be South American millionaires and took Angela's whole family to Buenos Aires for a holiday, but I suppose if you have got a name like Angela Delacourt things like that will automatically happen to you, and that is why I would not marry anybody called Bloggs or give my children sordid names. I always did have a weakness for gorgeous names, and little knew that on this trek I was going to meet a girl called—but you'd better wait for that, because as usual I am going too far ahead.

It turned out that Mrs. Folds had organised many successful pony treks before. She said the people she wanted were dependable kind of people and experienced riders who preferably hadn't been on a pony trek before. Because if they had been before they were apt to think they knew all about it and tell her how it should be run, and she got rather fed up at being told how much better organised the last one was.

29

She invited Ann and Miss Crombie and me to go to her house to talk things over. She said she had already got five people, including herself, and Ann and I and Miss Crombie made eight, and could we get four more to make up the dozen?

This rather knocked me for six, as I hadn't visualised Miss Crombie going at all. For one thing, she hadn't a pony. But Miss Crombie was very sold on the idea of going, and Mrs. Folds said, of course she must go and the brother who had the riding school would be delighted to lend her a pony, and Mrs. Folds had never had such a thrill in her life as on the day she watched Miss Crombie collect three cups at Richmond Horse Show—and by then my eyes were nearly dropping out because I hadn't any idea of Miss Crombie's glorious past, which just proves that you should never despise people because they don't choose to beef about how marvellous they are.

"Gosh, don't you think I'm a bit past it?" said Miss Crombie modestly, and Mrs. Folds said, "What rot," and Miss Crombie looked like the rising sun and said, "I daresay I'll be able to help with the ponies, even if I am a bit of a has been." I was absolutely knocked by this noble attitude, because I'm sure that if I won even one cup at Richmond Horse Show I'd spend the rest of my life with it hung round my neck so that nobody could jolly well miss it. But as you have probably noticed, people who are absolutely the top in any walk of life are always the humblest and the nicest.

Mrs. Folds said she would like to meet our ponies as well as us, so we went out and took a look at Black Boy and George on whom Ann and I had spent hours of patient labour before bringing them out.

I had Black Boy looking as if he was upholstered in patent leather, and if his hoofs were dusty it only

needed a flick of a duster to see that they were
polished underneath.

George, Ann's pony, had terrific looks and style,
and a very intelligent way of knowing when he was
due to be admired. The tack looked good too. We
stood smugly by, hoping that Mrs. Folds would think
we always maintained this standard of grooming. Of
course in a way we do, because I think that people
who let their ponies get that dusty, shabby look are
disgusting. How can ponies do their best when they
know they don't look nice? And they know all right.
I'll say they do.

She inspected those ponies like an eagle-eyed judge
at a top show. She asked us loads of questions. How
did we start our grooming? How did we finish it?
How did we use the various tools and brushes?

I think she wanted to make sure we knew our stuff
and hadn't just made a special effort for her benefit,
or even got somebody to do the ponies for us.

She asked us when and how often we cleaned our
tack, and Ann surprisingly said she did hers while
watching television, which shook Mrs. Folds who
asked, didn't she find that a bit difficult? and Ann
said, not at all when you got into the way of it and
didn't upset tins of polish into the cushions.

She then asked how and where Ann got George and
I got Black Boy. Well—that was a saga! Ann had had
a previous pony of great beauty and charm called
Seraphine, which Ann's mother in a soul-less moment
had sold because it threw Ann's little sister Pam. This
sad story is related in one of my previous books. As it
turned out, Seraphine went to a very good home with
a nice boy called Lewis, and on one occasion Ann had
the ghastly experience of being beaten in a jump-off
by Lewis on Seraphine, which you must admit was a

31

Gale Force Ten experience for anybody. All this now had to be told to Mrs. Folds in a condensed form, which wasn't very condensed either, as it took about half an hour.

As for where and how I got Black Boy! That is all written down in a book called *Jill's Gymkhana*, and if you haven't read it I can tell you that Black Boy cost me twelve pounds from a farmer who didn't want him, and when I bought him I couldn't even ride him and had nowhere to put him. How I learned to ride him and got a stable for him is part of the story. So telling Mrs. Folds all this took about another half-hour, and when it was finished she said that she thought both Ann and I had enterprise and weren't afraid of hard work, and were in fact the kind of people she liked to have on a pony trek.

As we ambled home along the grass verges, Ann said she hoped we weren't expected to keep up all this hard work and enterprise for ever or the pony trek wouldn't be much fun after all, and I said we'd be sure to have fun but we'd got to remember that this trek was also supposed to be educational from a horsy point of view, and by the time it was over we'd be practically fit to join the Canadian Mounties.

"Who are we going to ask?" I said. "She said four people." "Diana of course," said Ann. "And Jackie Heath—not Val, she's such a bighead—and Mercy Dulbottle and April Cholly-Sawcutt."

"Wow!" I said. "You're out on a cloud. Diana—yes. But Jackie won't come without Val, they always do everything together, and why on earth Mercy Dulbottle? She's hopeless. And April! Mrs. Folds would fall down dead at the sight of that fattie, never mind how awful she looks on a pony."

Ann said that Jackie would be quite glad to get

32

away from Val for once, and as for Mercy, that was strategy. Her aunt would be pleased for her to be invited, and might even give the Pony Club a field for winter jumping, which we badly needed.

"I'm positively certain she won't," I said glumly.

"But strategy often pays off," said Ann. "And here's some more. If we ask April to go, Captain Cholly-Sawcut will be pleased and he'll go on taking an interest in us. I wonder you didn't think of all that, with your mighty brain."

"H'm," I said. "You can try Jackie Heath, and I'll give you Mercy. But April! She'll wreck the trek and get sent home, and far from taking an interest in us Captain Cholly-Sawcutt will be furious. Besides, we don't want Mrs. Folds to think we've got nothing but weird friends. She may swallow Mercy, but April—oh murder! I vote we take Wendy Mead. She's older, and a super rider, and jolly nice."

"Okay, okay," said Ann. "I wonder who Mrs. Folds has asked? Supersonic people, I bet."

"They may try to make us look like kids," I said. "That's why it'll be a good thing to have somebody like Wendy Mead on our side. So we'll wash out April."

"If you say so," said Ann. "I'll go and ask Jackie and Mercy, and you can ask Diana and Wendy."

All Those Preparations

I RODE round to the Meads' farm that evening on Rapide, but when I got there I was so interested that I forgot what I had gone for.

They had put the new foal out to grass for the first time, and she was beautiful. The whole Mead family were out there, Mr. and Mrs. Mead and Wendy and Howard, and Aunt Poppy who had once been the Dairy Queen of Britain, and Charlie the stockman, and of course Babs who was only three and had shown her Shetland when she was only two. (At least she had sat on the Shetland, and the judge had given her third place to encourage her.)

Everybody was gazing at the lovely foal, a chestnut with a white blaze and three white socks. Her mother was a hunter called Stay Happy.

"I can just see our Babs winning the Horse of the Year Show on her in about fifteen years time," said Mrs. Mead.

"She'll be about past it by then," said Mr. Mead.

"Past it! She'll only be eighteen."

"I meant the filly. She'll be fifteen."

Wendy said she had seen a twenty-year-old horse jumping at Wembley on television, and everybody

argued for a bit, and by the time we had got Babs the first woman to win the Fred Foster Memorial Cup I had forgotten what I came for!

Mrs. Mead wanted to name the foal Always Happy, but Wendy said that was simply asking for trouble. No pony could be always happy, and it might put her off winning anything ever. Aunt Poppy said, why not call her Always Sad, and then she'd probably win all the time and it would be interesting?

Howard said, what about Always Hoping which sounded optimistic? Charlie the stockman said that sounded as if the poor thing knew it would never get anywhere, and Mr. Mead said, why Always anything? He believed in a good honest name for a horse, like Black Rock for a colt and Brown Alice for a filly.

Aunt Poppy said, as Babs was going to own and ride the filly why not let Babs choose the name? Babs thought a bit, and then said, "Teddy".

Wendy said, "That's a boy's name, silly," and I stuck my oar in and said, "What about Teddy Beverley of the Beverley Sisters?" and Babs said, "She's called Teddy," and stamped a bit.

"Now that's enough of that!" said Mrs. Mead.

I remembered what I had come for and told them.

"Oh, I'd love to go," said Wendy. "But I can't. There's too much to do—they can't do without me here."

"Nonsense," said Mr. Mead. "It'll do you good to have a holiday, Wendy, and you deserve one. It's only for a week, and we'll manage, won't we, Mother?"

Mrs. Mead was equally keen for Wendy to go, so it was settled.

I then went home and rang up Diana Bush, who had already heard about the pony trek and was just waiting to be asked to go.

"Who else is going from here?" she said.

"Wendy," I said. "And Ann's out now asking Jackie Heath and—well—er—Mercy Dulbottle."

"Gosh!" Diana screamed. "Mercy? What for?"

I explained that it was strategic, and Diana said hopefully that perhaps Mercy wouldn't want to go, but having been invited both she and her aunt would feel flattered, so we would get the field and also be able to invite somebody else—preferably a close friend of Diana's—to go on the trek, and that would be killing two birds with one stone.

But at that very moment Ann came in with her news.

"No go," I said to Diana. "Mercy's coming." And I rang off.

"She was thrilled to be asked," said Ann. "So was her aunt thrilled about Mercy being asked, which is the main point. The things we do for the Pony Club! Jackie was thrilled, too."

"I hope Mercy rides something the right size for her," I said gloomily, "instead of just letting her stirrup leathers down till her feet brush the daisies."

"Oh, her aunt's going to see she's well turned out. I mentioned that. I think of everything."

Next morning we each received a letter from Mrs. Folds with a list of what we had to take with us for the trek. It was to be a real trek, with no prepared meals awaiting our arrival. We would buy our own food and cook it when we needed to, and we each had to carry an emergency meal such as a tin of lunch meat, some cheese sections, and a few apples.

"That's in case we get lost in the desert," said Ann.

"What desert?" I asked hopefully, and Ann said she really meant some wild moor, like in *Lucy Gray*. I pointed out that Lucy Gray fell into a snowbound river in mid-winter and didn't die of starvation in a desert in August, and Ann said, "You know what I mean. Do we have to argue about every little thing?"

"Look at this list," I said. "There are about four million things down on it. It says, 'sleeping-bag, pillow slip with small pillow in it if required'—I shan't bother—'rug, yes. Two towels, toilet articles'—that's tooth-brush and soap and such. 'Change of underwear, socks, shoes, and shirt. Pyjamas, mack. Spare tack, cleaning materials, grooming tools. Cup, saucer, two plates, preferably aluminium for lightness. Knife, fork, spoon of picnic type'. What's picnic type?—oh, I know, plastic, only the forks break if you dig them into anything tough. Then it says in big letters, 'Do not forget handkerchiefs and first-aid kit.' Then we go back to small letters, and it says, 'The above articles should be carried in saddle-bags. Cooking utensils will be carried by a pack pony. Travel in slacks, shirt, and light sweater, and bring jodhpurs and jacket.' "

I hadn't used my saddle-bags for ages and couldn't remember where they were, so I made a wild search and turned out every cupboard in the cottage, and Mummy said, "You can just put all that back! The kitchen looks like a shambles."

I mumbled, "I can't find my saddle-bags," and rushed out to the stable and turned all the tack upside down, and they weren't there. Eventually I found them under a stack of old newspapers in the garden shed, and they were smothered in cobwebs and had become a home for a family of beetles, so they had to be bashed and beaten and scrubbed, and I had to take them down to the saddler's for new straps.

I should have thought the list of instructions was perfectly straightforward, but as you know, there are some people who can't understand "the cat sat on the mat". Mercy Dulbottle rang up in a Force Eight flap. When it said, "travel in slacks, shirt, and light sweater" did it mean we had got to wear a sweater even if it was very hot? And did it matter what colour of rug she took? And oughtn't she to take a dressing-gown, and weren't we going to wear dresses at all?

I gave a hollow groan and said, "Just *think*! And if you want to take your entire wardrobe with you, you can always have the pony pulling a light cart."

Ann who could hear every word of this bright conversation then grabbed the phone and said, "I'm taking a Red Indian set I had when I was seven."

"Now you've done it," I said. "She'll think you mean it. She'll probably bring the Air Hostess set she had when she was six."

Gradually we all got ready, after a lot of meetings and conferences and arguments. Jackie Heath said it looked as if the three pounds ten that we were paying was going to feed the ponies and not us. She had had visions of rolling up each night to some cosy farm-house and tucking in to a sumptuous meal with a Doris Archer-type farmer's wife whanging out the jam pancakes, and she took a poor view of hotting up our own cans of stew over a smokey camp fire and making tea in the saucepan which had warmed last night's onions.

Ann told Jackie not to go round talking like that, as her mother—Ann's—had the Doris Archer idea herself and mustn't be told the horrible truth, or she might stop Ann going even at the last moment.

Then Mrs. Folds rang up. Would our party go over there and meet her party?

"I expect they'll be hard-riding, experienced trekkers," I said. "I hope they are. Because it means their fires won't smoke and their tea won't taste of onions.

We'll be able to leave all the toil to them. They'll love knocking up hearty meals in the dripping depths of the forest while we pretend we can't do a thing."

Ann said, "Oh, come off it. Next minute you'll be lolling in a sleeping-bag while some experienced trekker brings your breakfast to bed. That'll be the day."

We arranged to meet at the cross-roads to ride over to Mrs. Folds' place. Jackie Heath turned up on a spirited pony called London Pride. He wore leg bandages and it was as much as she could do to hold him. He curvetted all over the place. Jackie hung on, and showed off.

"Crumbs!" I said. "What do you think this is—bloodstock sales?"

"Any minute now," said Ann, "you'll go into orbit."

London Pride did a quick pirouette and backed into Black Boy.

"Here—lay off!" I said, annoyed. There are always some people who like to ride ponies who are just a bit too much for them, and think it clever, whereas it just makes trouble for other people, which isn't horsemanship.

"He's all right when he's moving," said Jackie. "It's just that he hates standing still. Who are we waiting for? Oh, Mercy, of course. She *would* be late."

Then Mercy appeared, sitting up very stiffly on her aunt's very valuable, dignified grey horse, Trifle. Ann, Wendy, Diana, and I were riding the ponies we intended to take on the trek, which seemed sensible. Trifle was so perfect that you felt if he got a speck of dust on him or trod on anything squelchy he'd fall down dead.

We set off along the lanes, which mostly had grass verges, with Ann and me leading, then Mercy on the exquisite Trifle, then Diana and Wendy, and Jackie

40

prancing in the rear which was the best place for London Pride. If he did swivel round and bolt he'd bolt back home, and not lame somebody else's pony.

We got to Mrs. Folds' place without any mishaps, and opened the gates and rode into the stable yard at the back, whereupon London Pride started doing a spot of rock and roll.

Mrs. Folds came running out of the house.

"Good grief!" she said in sharp ringing tones. "I hope *that* one isn't intending to go on the trek. You'd better dismount and get him under control, whoever you are."

Jackie looked as if she was going to break her wrists, but she got down and managed to tie London Pride out of reach of the other ponies.

"I'm perfectly able to control him," she said.

"I wouldn't count on that," said Mrs. Folds. "He's a show ring animal, and he certainly isn't going out on the open road with me. Haven't you got another?"

"I ride him regularly," said Jackie, sticking to her dignity. "I brought him out because he needs a lot of exercise and I like riding something that needs riding. Actually I've got a hill pony called Marmion to take on the trek. Quite a slug."

I butted in and started introducing everybody before war broke out.

"Haven't *you* got another one?" said Mrs. Folds, looking at Mercy. "That grey is much too good for trekking, and too valuable."

"Oh, yes, I have," blurted Mercy. "Trifle belongs to my aunt and never goes anywhere rough, only I didn't want you to think I was a mess right from the start."

We all began to giggle and Mercy looked as if she was going to cry.

Mrs. Folds said hastily, "Well, all tie up, and then

41

come along in and meet your fellow trekkers." She looked sternly at Jackie. "I'll get one of the men to walk your animal about before anything gets wrecked."

We all went into the house, and just as I was crossing the doorstep a frightful thought clonked into my burning brain.

"Wow!" I muttered. "Oh, Christmas!"

"What's up?" said Ann.

"We've forgotten Miss Crombie."

We're Actually Going

WE had indeed done that dreadful thing. In making the arrangements we had told Jackie and Mercy and Wendy and Diana where to meet and at what time, to go to Mrs. Folds, and not one of us had given a single thought to Miss Crombie. She might not have existed. Actually I hadn't thought of Miss Crombie for days.

I stood rooted on that doorstep.

"What's the matter?" said Mrs. Folds.

I blurted out, "I forgot all about Miss Crombie."

"That's a bad show, isn't it?" said Mrs. Folds. "You'd better go back and fetch her, hadn't you?"

I dashed out and untied Black Boy. In no time we were pelting along the lanes. He didn't see the point of all this hurry, and tried to play up a bit.

Eventually we arrived at Miss Crombie's house, and I hadn't decided what to say. It was going to be awkward. I couldn't possibly tell her we'd forgotten her.

I slid down, tied Black Boy to the garden railings —he was blowing hard and glowering at me—and rushed up to the door and rang the yellow bell. Nobody came, there wasn't a sound. She's out, I thought. that's torn it.

The next-door neighbour came out of her house and said, "Do you want Miss Crombie? She's in bed, I'm afraid. You can open the door and go upstairs. It's the first room at the top. Knock, and say who you are."

I shot into the house and up the stairs. I could hear Miss Crombie coughing. I knocked at the bedroom door and croaked, "It's Jill."

"Come in," said a dim voice.

Miss Crombie was sitting up in bed in a red dressing-gown and a pink hair net listening to Mrs. Dale's Diary. Mrs. Maggs or somebody was just saying, "It's me feet wot's killing me."

"Oh, Jill, I am so glad to see you," said Miss Crombie, switching off the radio as if she was glad to get rid of Mrs. Dale. "I've got a septic ear. It's nothing catching, but I shan't be able to go on the pony trek." She sounded as if she was going to cry.

"Oh, hard luck," I said. "I'm most frightfully sorry."

I really meant it. I hadn't realised how keen she was to go on the trek, and I could only think how disappointed I should have been myself.

"Actually," I said, "I came to fetch you round to Mrs. Folds' place. We're going to make final arrangements."

"Oh, dear!" said Miss Crombie, madly twisting the collar of the red dressing-gown. "I feel so miserable. It was going to be the nicest thing that happened to me for ages, and now it's all off."

"What ghastly luck," I said. "I say, is there anything I can get you?"

"Nothing at all," said Miss Crombie, sniffing frantically. "My neighbour is awfully kind and brings me meals—if you can call them meals, just

44

milky stuff that all tastes alike. It's just one of those things, and I'll have to put up with it."

I felt so sorry for her and very guilty too. I wished I had been more thoughtful and gone to see her before.

"I do wish you were going," I said, and I meant that too.

"I'll be thinking about you," she said, "and picturing you trekking and having wonderful times. This is the worst thing that's happened to me since my pony took a chunk out of the judge's sleeve when I was thirteen and he was just going to place me first in the showing class."

"Oh, what happened?"

"He was touchy and placed me third, and he said that little girls oughtn't to show vicious ponies. Topsy wasn't vicious, only she hated men with red moustaches, only I couldn't tell him that." She dragged out a terrific sigh. "Well, I won't keep you, I expect you're dying to get to Mrs. Folds'. It was awfully nice of you to come."

"They'll be frightfully sorry about you, when I tell them." I said. This was probably a slight exaggeration, but it seemed to make Miss Crombie happier.

"Just explain," she said, suddenly producing a smile. "And say I'll be with them in spirit."

This extraordinary remark sounded more than weird to me. I found myself imagining a ghostly form which was a sort of cross between Miss Crombie and Lady Di, floating along beside me on a phantom steed, and it was a bit putting-off. I mean, think of having to look right through Miss Crombie just when you were taking off to jump a fence!

However, I said good-bye, and pelted back to Mrs. Folds' place like the "I galloped, Dirk galloped, we galloped all three" man in the poem who brought the good news from somewhere to somewhere else.

"Miss Crombie's got a bad ear," I said. "She can't come on the trek."

"Oh, that's rugged," said Mrs. Folds. "Well, come along in and meet the other four people who are going."

The first people I saw were two very neat-looking sisters with whiter-than-white blouses and pony tail hair-dos.

"These are Katy and Billie Smith," said Mrs. Folds.

I said "Hallo" and so did they.

"And this is Rosevale Washington."

Oooh! What a gorgeous name! I thought. Rosevale was tall and thin and had platinum blond hair, and looked exactly like the girls in western films. She was American, and her father was at a U.S. base not far from Chatton.

"Hiya!" she said with a friendly wave.

"Cheerio," I said.

"And this," went on Mrs. Folds, "is April Cholly-Sawcutt."

"Oh, *crumbs*!" I said.

April was grinning at me like a slice of melon.

"How did you get here?" I said.

"We're very proud to have Captain Cholly-Sawcutt's daughter with us," said Mrs. Folds.

You wait, I thought. Just you wait!

"Daddy's retired from show jumping now," said April. "He's on the B.S.J.A. board, so if you want any of the rules altering, now's your chance."

She looked fatter than ever, just like a cottage loaf in pink denim jeans and a yellow sweater, if you can imagine that.

"So everybody knows everybody," said Mrs. Folds.

46

"All sit down on the floor. I want to have a word about rules on this trek. Actually there aren't any. I take it for granted you'll behave yourselves and use your common sense. Remember that most of you are Pony Club members, and anything you do out of turn is scored up by onlookers against the Pony Club. They don't know you personally, and if they see any bad behaviour they say, 'Huh! So that's Pony Club manners.' So keep the party clean. I give the orders, and you do exactly as I say without arguing or beefing. Understand?"

"We don't know where we're going yet," somebody piped.

"You soon will," said Mrs. Folds. "Plenty of moorland and some sea-coast."

"Whoopee!" said April. "I love riding ponies in the sea. Once I nearly got drowned."

Mrs. Folds said that was no recommendation, and everybody started gabbling at once. April wasn't squashed, she was unsquashable.

Then came the day when the ponies left in horse vans, and we were to follow next morning by train and connect with them.

You can imagine the scene at dawn at Pool Cottage where I dwell. The night before I set my alarm clock for five and then got scared it wouldn't go off and borrowed Mummy's alarm clock too. Mrs. Crosby, our helpful daily, said sarkily, would I care for hers as well?

I said, bring them all along just to be on the safe side, and she said, "That's the first time you've ever talked about the safe side, you're getting old before your time and no wonder with all those ponies shaking up your bones," and Mummy said, "Oh, for goodness' sake! You've still got your yellow shirt to iron, Jill, and don't say you'll do it in the morning because there won't be time, there never is."

At least I was grateful for the fact that my mother is not the kind of one who when you are going anywhere tells you fifty-nine-thousand times to be careful.

I went to bed with three alarm clocks ticking off-beat all round me, but actually I never needed them. I woke up at four and didn't bother to go to sleep again. I got up and dressed in old clothes, and made my bed and tidied my room so as to leave no ill feelings about me after I'd gone, and then I crept downstairs in the somewhat gloomy half-light and brewed a cup of cocoa and started on Black Boy's brush-up and feed.

Rapide glowered at me sleepily. I felt sad to leave him behind, but I had arranged for Mrs. Darcy to have him and I knew he'd enjoy it.

Then I went in to dress properly, and stole up the stairs like a burglar, but I needn't have bothered, as during my absence all three alarm clocks had gone off like bombs—one starting as the other stopped—and Mummy had had a rude awakening.

At long last everything was ready, and we all met at the train. I was sorry for Ann, because she was the only one whose mother insisted on coming to see her off and stood there saying, "Now do be careful," until the train was actually on the move.

The First Day

WE were all excited and behaved rather madly on the train, but it didn't matter as we had two carriages to ourselves.

"So this is really it!" I thought, as we finally reached our destination, which was the yard of an old-fashioned inn called The Woodpecker in an old English village whose name I forget.

The ponies had arrived, including the pack pony, and were standing about looking surprised but happy in the sharp yellow sunshine. They had been slightly bewildered, we were told, when they came out of the vans and were probably expecting to see a show ring, but when they recognised their owners they started tossing their heads, jingling bits, and whiffling happily.

Then we had to sort out the saddle-bags and start buckling up. Mrs. Folds was very particular. The rugs had to be folded exactly corner to corner and then over again, and she made some people do this about three times before she was satisfied.

"This is worse than Judge's Inspection," said Diana, settling her kit for about the fourth time. "I hope it isn't going on all the time, or we'll do nothing else but arrange saddle-bags prettily and without unsightly bulges, as she calls them."

"You'll soon get the idea that it's as easy to put things on straight as crooked," said Mrs. Folds cheerfully. "Good gracious, April, what have you got there? You're not going to ride with your arms full!"

"It's only food," said April. "It won't go in my saddle-bags."

"It looks like a whole grocer's shop. I only said food for one meal, you know."

"It only is for one meal," grumbled April, and Jackie Heath screamed and said, "Whatever is it?"

"There's only a lump of cold beef," said April, "and a treacle pudding—it's the basin that makes it bulgy—and a fruit cake and cheese and some bananas and buttered rolls—oh, and a few sandwiches, and some apples and a tin of peaches, and some mint lumps, and I think I put a tin of spaghetti in—I can't remember—and a few odds and ends. So stop beefing, all of you, because you might be glad of this if we get lost on the moors. You'll be imploring me to share it out when you're starving and I'm jolly well the only one that's got any food."

"I should say the pony will do the beefing," said Billie Smith. "Fancy having to carry saddle-bags and *that* load and you as well!"

"Don't be rude or you won't get anything," said April. "Not if you're dying even. And Ricky's a tough pony."

"He'll need to be," said Wendy.

Rosevale Washington had come on a long-legged, wiry pony called Sikey. At least that's what I thought she was called, but it turned out afterwards to be Psyche, which is the name of a Greek goddess, which I always thought was pronounced Fish.

"Have any of you done any trekking before?" she asked. We all said we hadn't, and had she?

51

She said she had done it in Texas, which was about as big as Europe, and where you could ride for a hundred miles without seeing anything but the wild.

Mercy Dulbottle said, "Were you ever shot at—like in western films?" And Rosevale said, only once and that was accidental, two G-men were out hunting a bank robber and thought she was it, and fired across her to make her stop, and then rode up and explained and apologised.

April said, "How tame? Why didn't you fire back?" and Mercy said, "I'd have been terrified, I'd have died."

I said to Rosevale, "I think your name is smashing," and she said, "Well, practically anything goes with Washington, and if anybody makes a crack about am I related to George, I'm not, and I'll murder them."

She then told us that she had three sisters, and all four of them were called after the places where they had been born, Rosevale in Texas, Altona in Idaho, Shelby also in Texas, and Bronx in New York.

Diana said, "I don't believe you. Nobody could possibly be called Bronx," and Rosevale said, "Cross my heart it's true." Her mother had said it was a pity, but once she'd started she couldn't stop.

Diana said, what if Bronx had been born in Kalamazoo? And before Rosevale could think up an answer to that one, Mrs. Folds came up and said, "Are you girls ever going to get organised? Rosevale, your saddle is much too far forward. You're not a jockey. Move it."

The innkeeper's wife came out and said, would the young ladies like a nice cup of hot coffee before they started off, because there was some ready.

We all shrieked, "Oh, yes, please!" as it was hours

since we had got up in the chilly dawn and some people had been too excited to eat any breakfast.

Mrs. Folds hesitated and then said, "Just this once, then, but in future we only eat while trekking, not in hotels."

We piled into the coffee room and had hot coffee and big fat buns. When we came out we saw a young man with a large camera wandering about among the ponies. He said he was a photographer from the local paper, and could he take some pictures of us, please.

"Oh, Mrs. Folds, do let him!" we all chorused, and she said, "All right, but do let's hurry up about it. I suppose we shall get away before tonight if we're lucky. Get mounted, everybody."

Perhaps you can guess what it is like making twelve ponies stand still and all face the same way at once. Chaos. After ten minutes of backing and turning round at the wrong minute we were all reduced to helpless mirth, and Mrs. Folds said to the photographer, "You'd better seize the moment and take a snap and hope for the best."

So he did, and of course there were cries of, "Oh, I wasn't in it at all," and "April's pony shoved mine out."

Everybody wanted to know when the paper with the photograph would be out, and how could we get some, and Mrs. Folds had to find the address of the farm where we should probably be, and we all had to find fourpence for a copy and postage, and it looked as if we should be at the Woodpecker Inn for life. Especially as Mrs. Woodpecker, or whatever she was called, then came out and said it was nearly half-past twelve, and would we care to stay for lunch?

"This is no good," said Mrs. Folds, firmly. "We're *not* having lunch here. Girls, you must stop all this

53

lunacy, we're starting at once whether you're ready or not. We'll buy some food in the village and eat it when we get into the country."

We went clattering in fine style through the small town where everybody stared at us, and at the end of the street Mrs. Folds and Wendy went into a shop and bought bread and cheese and fruit and half-pint bottles of milk, and straws.

Leaving the houses and shops behind there ran ahead a hard metal road which the ponies didn't like at all, but at last we came to a side road with a signpost, "Mitchley in the Moor $6\frac{1}{2}$ miles."

"Doesn't it sound lovely?" said Ann. "Like cottages and orchards."

"Hope you're right," said Diana. "Could be two dirty farms and a dump."

I was enjoying the feeling of the sun on my back. The road curved upwards towards a ridge of hills, and soon when we looked back over our shoulders we could see the place we had left behind, the squiggle of streets and toy-sized houses and a church tower and a gas works, and a canal with two barges like moving dots. Just like a model village on a table top.

"Oh, I am hot," said April, panting up beside me. "I wish we could go into some woods."

"There aren't any in sight," said Ann. "But think of the lovely cool heathery smell when we get to the moors."

"I could do with some lovely cool heathery lunch," grumbled April.

"What about all that food you're carrying?"

"Oh, I've had some of that. But I don't want to eat it all at once. Gosh, it's half-past one."

"Let's pretend we're Jacobites fleeing from the cursed soldiers of King George," said Diana. "Whist!

Are we pursued? Or have we perchance thrown them off?"

"Oh, get lost!" said April. "Anybody would think you were six."

"What April doesn't appreciate," said Wendy, "is that we're actually doing what we've been longing for, pony trekking. It's utterly marvellous."

"What's the matter back there?" called Mrs. Folds, rising in her stirrups and looking back.

"Some of them think they're dying of starvation back here," said Wendy.

"We'll get to the top of the hill," said Mrs. Folds, "and then we'll stop if we can find the right sort of place."

The sky was blue with a few cotton-wool clouds, the breeze stirred the ponies' manes, and there was a kind of smell of freedom in the air.

Aren't we lucky? I thought. And then I pictured all the people sitting in offices and standing in shops, and driving buses along crowded streets and doing chores in houses.

Soon we would be coming out upon level moorland to find a green clearing waiting for us among the heather.

But when we got to the top of the hill it wasn't like that at all. There wasn't even any heather, just some thin waste land with coarse grass and wire fences and staring sheep.

So we rode on looking for a better place. Then we came to gates across the road, one after the other. Somebody had to get down each time and open the gate and shut it behind us. This wasn't a popular job at all.

"I've gone weak," said Rosevale, hauling herself

back on to her pony. "If I have to do this again I'll die of exhaustion right here in the roadway."

"Oh, please, Mrs. Folds, let's stop," said Katy Smith. "We could sit on those stones where there's some bracken."

"All right," she said. "Everybody down."

We loosened the ponies' girths and tied them to the fence posts and flopped thankfully into the bracken, from whence rose up a cloud of pestering flies. The ponies stamped and looked miserable, and we slapped and said, "Get away, you horrible little beasts"—to the flies.

But the food tasted marvellous, when you got used to sharing it with the flies. The big bread rolls disappeared like magic with chunks of cheese. Home seemed far away and it was all adventurous and independent.

"At least we're right at the top of the world," said Ann. "We shan't have to do any more climbing this afternoon, but I do hope it gets a bit more heathery."

"Oh, you've got heather on the brain," I said, and I tore out a waving branch of bracken and started bashing her with it. That set everybody off, and soon we were all bashing away and getting ourselves boiling hot.

"That's enough of that," said Mrs. Folds in the end. "Now you can make a tidy pile of all this torn bracken. We can't leave the countryside in a mess. Pick up all those sweet papers and bits, please."

"You can't really call this the countryside," said Billie Smith. "It's a mess to start with, and the bracken was too high anyway. In about a week it would have been all over the road and somebody would have had to spend hours cutting it back. We've done all that for them. They ought to give us medals."

"You've ·got an answer for everything. Hurry up now."

So we collected all our rubbish and buried it and cleared up generally.

"A little of these hard roads goes a long way with me," grumbled Jackie Heath. "They don't do the ponies' feet any good. We'll be working on them for hours tonight getting stones out of their beastly little hoofs. Gosh, I hope we get to some turf."

"I thought your Marmion was a marvellous hill pony who could stride up the rocky slopes of mountains and all that," said Ann sarkily.

"He doesn't mind rocky slopes, it's tarmac he draws the line at, and so does yours," said Jackie. "Look at the brute now, pecking with his off fore. I bet he's got a stone in."

"George isn't a brute," said Ann.

"Yes he is, technically."

"Oh, drop dead!" said Ann, going over to examine George's hoofs, which luckily proved to be clean.

At last we moved off, and we hadn't gone far when we got our wish, we were out on real moorland with turf under foot and heather all round.

"All we want now is a few skylarks," said Billie Smith who was inclined to be poetical.

"What for?" said April, who wasn't.

Billie said she was going to write a poetical account of the trek and she wanted to put in a line about "the skylark soaring from the ling" and she felt she couldn't if it wasn't strictly true.

"But poetry doesn't have to be strictly true, that's the whole point of it," I said. "I should stick that line in anyway, it sounds good."

"What's ling?" said April.

57

"Heather, you clot. What do you make it rhyme with, Billie?"

"Thing," said Billie. " 'And piping like a crazy thing'."

"That's rotten poetry," said Diana. "Why don't you put, 'Just listen to the little thing.' That's heaps better."

"You'd better write the Poetical Trek instead of Billie," I said.

"There was a young poet called Billie," chanted April, "whose poems were awfully silly—ouch!"

Billie had leaned sideways and grabbed April by the neck and they both came to the ground.

"None of that," said Wendy. "You two are going the right way to get sent home."

"Wouldn't it be *nice*," said Ann, "if there were only *nice* people on this trek like me and Wendy and Jill."

"Wait till I get you!" said Diana.

Black Boy was trotting along in a state of bliss, with pricked ears. I patted his glossy neck for sheer joy, I could tell how much he was enjoying himself. As for me, I wouldn't have changed places with anybody in the world, and that is saying something, because when I am doing dreary chores I can think of a thousand people I would change places with and I expect you can too.

We had got a mistress at school called Miss Deacon, and she was always setting this gruesome subject for an essay, "If you were not yourself who would you rather be?" which I think shows little imagination when there are so many more interesting subjects to write essays about. Then when people said what they really thought, like wanting to be Haley Mills or Pat Smythe, she told us off for not wanting to be somebody worthy but obscure like the matron of an orphanage or a noble leper nurse.

"Look at Mercy's pony," said Ann. "Isn't he limping?"

"I've noticed that for a quite a time," said Diana. "I wondered why she didn't do anything about it."

"Does Mercy ever do anything about anything?"

"Hi, Mercy!" I sang out. "Isn't Pippin limping?"

"I'm afraid so," said Mercy in a worried sort of way. "Only I didn't want to hold everybody up."

"You dope, we'll be held up for good if he goes really lame. Let's have a look."

Mercy got down and so did I and Ann.

"He's lost a shoe," said Ann. "When did that happen?"

By now everybody had stopped and Mrs. Folds came back.

"Now what's wrong?"

We explained.

"Really, Mercy," she said. "Did you examine the pony's shoes before you sent him off yesterday?"

"One of the men saw to it," said Mercy going red.

Mrs. Folds rolled her eyes and made a face.

"Look, my child. Just because your aunt has stables and employs people to look after the horses, that isn't the slightest excuse for you. A real horsewoman never 'leaves it to the men' without checking. What were you doing?"

Mercy looked as if she was going to wilt away.

"I suppose I overslept," she said. "And when I woke up the pony had gone and I thought it would be all right. I never thought about shoes being loose or anything like that. Have I got to go back and look for it?"

"Help! We'd be here a week," said Mrs. Folds. "How long has the pony been limping?"

"I don't really know," said Mercy sniffing madly. "I wasn't noticing."

"Gosh, you've got something to learn about trekking."

"What do you want us to do, Mrs. Folds?" asked Wendy.

"We're only about half a mile from where we strike the road," said Mrs. Folds, "and there's a village. I don't dare to hope we'll find a smith there, but we may find somebody who can do something. After the village we've got to cover a mile of tarmac before we come to the field track. Mercy, you'll have to lead the pony carefully. One or two of you girls stay with her, and the rest of us will ride on to the village and scout about for help. If we can't find any, Mercy had better resign herself to staying there for life."

"Oh, this is awful, I've spoilt everything for everybody and I wish I was dead," said Mercy between sniffs, as the others rode on and Ann, Diana, and I stayed behind with her.

"Don't be idiotic," I said helpfully.

Diana of course had to rub it in by saying, "People who don't examine their pony's shoes are the gruesome depths."

"Oh, dear, Pippin's trembling," said Mercy.

"If I was your pony I'd tremble," said Diana. "I'd tremble from morning till night."

"Oh, drop dead!" I said to Diana. "It isn't a tragedy, Mercy, so do shut up about it. It's sure to turn out all right."

Mercy's spirits were usually about sea level and she was always getting into trouble. The first time I ever met her, we went out on a marsh to catch some ducks

belonging to her aunt and put them into a hut. After intense and bitter labours we kept whanging those ducks into the hut, only to find that Mercy had forgotten to shut the window at the other end and the birds were out again as fast as they went in.

You just had to get used to her.

So we trudged on, and at last we got to the village, though Ann and Diana would go on ragging Mercy, saying we'd probably have to leave her with some kind woman and pick her up a week later on our way back, till she was nearly weeping. Wendy came riding out to meet us.

"It's okay!" she yelled. "What on earth's the matter, Mercy? What have you squares been saying to her? Well, listen, it's the greatest luck. There's a farmer in the village who has a small forge and he'll fix Pippin up."

"Oh, really? Do you mean it?" said Mercy. "Oh, Wendy, you are marvellous." She dropped the reins, tripped over them, and fell flat on the ground.

"Better let me take Pippin," said Wendy. "Come along now, boy. It's all right."

We staggered into the village and found the others resting their ponies at a drinking fountain, and about twenty village children gathered round to stare at them, saying things like, "Please, miss, are you the circus?" and, "Is it going to be on telly?"

We had a long wait, as the farmer who put on the new shoe must have worked at a snail's pace, but in the end it was done, and when we were ready to start again, believe it or not, we couldn't find Mercy who eventually turned up in the grocery shop where she and April were stocking up with chocolate bars to make up for all that misery.

The Second Day

AT about five o'clock we arrived at the farm which was to be our first night stop.

It was a really farmy-looking farm, the sort of place you expect a farm to be. I mean, there are some farms which look like red brick houses on the roadside, with a few gruesomely clean sheds behind with tin roofs, and no sign of any animals, the poor things being deliberately kept out of view as if they'd spoil the effect.

But our farm was at the end of a leafy lane, and it was an old stone house with elm trees behind it, and currant bushes in the garden on which some washing was spread out, and there was an orchard at the side, with some lovely tumbledown outbuildings, and a really old-fashioned smelly farmyard. I mean, who doesn't absolutely adore smelly farmyards?

In the yard a lot of happy, free hens were pecking around, and three cats were stretched on the sun-warmed cobbles, and a sheepdog was frisking, and you could hear cows mooing in the shippon and pails clanking.

The sight of this gorgeous farm instantly made me decide that I would make farming my career.

The farmer's wife, who as you would expect was

large, colourful, and beaming, came out and said, "Welcome, everybody. Very, very glad to see you girls. There's two lofts ready for you to sleep, just like you wanted, and lots of clean straw, and our Bob has put up the barbecue in the orchard so you'll be able to get on with your cooking, and if you want anything don't be afraid to ask. We're here to please."

"Thank you, Mrs. Timmins," said Mrs. Folds. "Everything looks lovely and we're very glad to be here after our long day. Come along, girls. Ponies first. Get busy."

There was a field specially for the ponies, and when we had unsaddled and rubbed them down they were turned out into the soft lush grass where they stood in a daze of happiness, munching dreamily and enjoying the peaceful summer evening.

Mrs. Timmins had been asked to order food for us, and a boy came staggering along to the barbecue with it. It looked marvellous, loads of sausages were sizzling, and the smell made us all want to burst into song, in fact some did. After we had eaten all we could, we made coffee and sat lapping it out of beakers and talking over the events of the day. It seemed days, not just hours, since we left home. It had been a glorious feast, and when it was all over we lay on our backs in the orchard and sleepily tried to count the apples in the branches overhead.

"I call this the tops," said Ann. "I'd like to go on like this for the rest of my life."

"You couldn't count on it not raining for the rest of your life," I argued sleepily.

"Oh, don't be so *mere*!" said Ann.

Katy Smith and Mercy who were both wildflower collectors had gone into a huddle about a new kind of orchid that they'd found, and Jackie and Rosevale who were keen bird-watchers, were perfectly certain they'd seen a new type of plover and were discussing photographs of nests which they'd taken.

Mrs. Folds said, "Mrs. Timmins is kindly allowing you all to ring up home on her phone. Go and line up at the front door, and take your turns, and only one minute each, please, or it'll go on all night."

"Bags I first!" shrieked April.

"Somebody sit on her head," suggested Rosevale.

"Oh, let her go first and then we'll get rid of her," said Diana. "I'll stand over her with a dandy brush and if she goes on for more than a minute I'll bash her."

"I'd better warn you that the calls will cost you two shillings each," said Mrs. Folds.

"We can do it on the cheap," said Jackie. "Bargain sale. You ring your mother, Jill, and tell her to let the other mothers know."

"I like that!" I said. "My two bob, I suppose?"

"We could all give you about threepence or fourpence."

Ann said she didn't think her mother would stand for a second-hand call, so in the end she and I between us did the ringing up for most of our party.

"Hallo, Mummy!" I chanted. "It's Jill. I'm still alive."

"What sort of a time are you having?" Mummy asked.

"Absolutely terrific. Marvellous. Utterly diggish. We had a smashing supper in the orchard. The farmer's wife is awfully kind."

Mummy said that sounded just fine, and in case I was worrying (which I wasn't) she wasn't a bit lonely because she was getting on like wildfire with her new book.

I said I would have to get off the line now, as about

six more people were waiting, and would she mind ringing Wendy's mother, and Jackie's mother and Diana's mother to say they were all right, but it was two shillings to ring and say so, and we were having a sort of economy drive.

Then it was Ann's turn and I could hear Mrs. Derry asking her if the food was perfectly clean and wholesome, and she did think we ought to have arranged to have properly served meals, not just scraping raw potatoes out of the ground and gnawing them, or whatever it was we did.

She then asked what we had had for supper, and Ann said that actually we had gnawed some greenish apples out of the orchard (which we had, and spat them out) and Mrs. Derry nattered a bit, and said, "What are the beds like, I insist on you telling me?" and Ann just said, "I'll have to ring off now as people are waiting, goodnight, Mummy," and cut off Mrs. Derry's shrieks by putting the receiver down, which proves what a wonderful thing the telephone is.

Next, we all went up into the twin lofts to inspect where we were going to sleep. We had to climb a ladder to get up there. There was a delicious smell of warm clean hay, and the bare boards were piled with fresh straw.

We got out our sleeping-bags, and in spite of most people saying they didn't want to go to bed yet, we were all awfully tired and began to settle down. Through the open window of the loft I could see dusk stealing over the sky and one star above the chimneys of the farm. Somewhere far off a cow moo-ed and a dog barked, then all was silent. My last thought was, "Another gorgeous day to come tomorrow."

It seemed only five minutes when I was awakened from a lovely dream in which I was being presented with a silver cup at the Horse of the Year Show and noticed that it was full of hot sausages which struck me as odd but pleasant. Somebody was pulling me about.

"Go away," I said. "I want to go to sleep."

"You mean you want to get up," said Ann's repulsively cheerful voice. "Get moving, you lazy thing. It's half-past six and the sun's shining like mad."

"It can't be," I said, pushing a wisp of hay off my nose.

"You can thank goodness you're not one of the cooks," said Ann. "Mrs. Folds had them up and cracking half an hour ago. You and I are supposed to be with her on foot inspection."

I shot up in the sleeping-bag, feeling a bit like a mermaid about the legs.

"There's nothing wrong with my feet."

"Ponies' feet, you dope. After Mercy's effort yesterday she's taking no chances. And she's on the warpath already. She found a stone in Katy's pony's hoof that Katy ought to have detected last night, and that kid's in the doghouse all right. Now we've got to examine *all* the feet."

"Where do we wash?" I asked.

"Same as last night, fetch the water from the pump and wash in the laundry."

Fifteen minutes later, in slacks and sweater I chased Ann down to the field where the ponies stood whisking their tails and looking ready for anything.

"I've found another stone," said Mrs. Folds grimly. "One of you tell April to come here."

April had had it! By this time I wouldn't have been surprised to find a stone in each of Black Boy's hoofs, except that I had examined them as a matter of course before leaving him the previous night.

67

April got a frightful talking to.

"I can see," said Mrs. Folds, "that before we go any further I shall have to give you a short, sharp talk about the care of your ponies. Carelessness is as bad as neglect, and some of you don't seem to have a clue. Just remember that your pony's comfort is much more important than your own. For one thing, remember that he can't tell you what's the matter, for another, he's too much of a gentleman to kick you which is what some of you deserve."

"Honestly, Ricky wasn't a bit lame last night," said April.

"I should jolly well hope he wasn't," said Mrs. Folds. "Come on, now, let's see what we're getting for breakfast."

Breakfast turned out to be just about the best meal I had ever eaten. It tasted so good in the cool but sparkling morning, and I expect you think I am yakking on and on about food, but if ever you go trekking yourself you will understand. The farm had provided bacon and eggs galore, and the three cooks, Wendy, Mercy, and Rosevale, had cooked them to a turn, and made toast over the glowing barbecue fire, and simply sloshed butter on it, and brewed gallons of tea.

"I vote we make these people cooks for the whole trek," said Diana, chasing a drop of bacon fat round her chin with her tongue.

"Do you mind!" said Wendy. "We like to be waited on, too, occasionally."

"Where are we going today, Mrs. Folds?" asked Jackie. "Wouldn't it be rather a good idea to go for a long ride and come back here tonight? I mean, it's so jolly nice here and the food's so jolly good."

"No go," said Mrs. Folds. "This is a trek. We press

on regardless. It's been nice here, but there are other nice places to come. You want to see a lot of different country, don't you? And you bird-watchers and wildflower fanciers want snapshots and specimens to take home. So the washers-up can get busy now, and the rest see to it that you leave this orchard and the lofts where you slept as tidy as you found them. Then collect your stuff and saddle up. Jill, will you come and help me with the pack pony?"

It took ages to get everybody ready. Wendy said, if it took as long as this for soldiers to leave a bivouac the war would be over before they got there.

People's tack was mixed up.

April was struggling wildly with her saddle. "It must have swelled in the night," she screamed. "And the stirrup leathers have stretched, they're miles long."

"That's my saddle you've got," moaned Mercy.

"Well, where's mine?" howled April, looking in a very sinister way at Jackie who had already mounted and was ready for off.

"I haven't got it!" snapped Jackie. "Where did you put it last night, you goof?"

"Oh, gosh, I think I must have got it," said Billie Smith. "I've got a jolly funny one, anyway."

"What you kids ought to do is label every single piece of tack," said Rosevale. "You're just not hep."

Mrs. Folds said, "You've only taken an hour and a half to water the ponies and another half-hour to saddle up. This is charming! What about a bit of an effort now?"

At last we were all ready, and Mrs. Timmins nearly wept when she said good-bye, you would think she had known us for years, and kept saying, "Come again soon. And if you're not comfortable where you're going, just come along back here."

And we were actually riding off and making a beautiful, horsemanlike exit, when Katy Smith discovered that she hadn't got her mack and had to go back for it amid groans and insults.

We left by a winding lane, the ponies trotting gently with pricked ears, and a light wind blowing our hair and bringing a fresh scent of morning in the country. Soon we came to a long wooded valley, and there on a small hill stood a ruined castle.

"Oh, I say, look!" cried Ann who was crazy about historical places. "Isn't it smashing? I wonder who lived there in the past?"

"My ancestors did," said Diana. "They were cattle thieves, and they had the place packed out with stolen cattle. That's why it's such a ruin, the cattle kicked the walls down trying to get out."

"What happened to your ancestors in the end?" said Katy Smith, who was the sort of person who believes everything. "Were they caught?"

"No, they all got murdered," said Diana. "Everybody who lived in castles got murdered in those days."

"Let's go and have a look inside," said Jackie, turning her pony to the slope.

We all rode up into the ruins, but there was nothing to see but crumbling walls and a bit of staircase and the remains of the keep. We played about a bit, and Katy found an old bone which she said must have been part of one of Diana's ancestors but it looked more like a sheep's leg to me.

So we rode on, singing as we went, and the ponies were as gay as we were. All the morning we rode through the woods, only we had to keep stopping every time Jackie and Rosevale thought they heard a new kind of bird chirping, and also to pick various flowers for Katy and Mercy. And of course everybody was taking snaps every time we stopped.

"What's this—a pony trek or a photographic society?" said Mrs. Folds laughing.

"I wish I had a ciné camera," said April. "Then I could take a film of the whole trek and when we get home everybody would pay to come and see it."

"That's what you think!" said Wendy.

"Well, I'm going to ask Daddy to buy me a ciné camera, and it'll do for about five birthdays and Christmases."

"You'll want a projector too," I said. "They're expensive."

"I'd borrow somebody's," said April, never at a loss.

At a farm we bought new bread which was still warm, and cheese and apples and milk for lunch, and took them back into the woods to eat. The woman at the farm filled our kettles for us too, and we built a fire in a fireplace made of stones, and brewed tea. There was a nearby stream rippling through the undergrowth and the ponies stood in it knee-deep and swished their tails at the flies. We all had a paddle after lunch, and Mercy brought out chocolate bars and divided them. It is very nice to munch chocolate and paddle at the same time.

In the afternoon we began to climb into the hills. Sometimes we had to dismount and lead the ponies over steep, rough bits. It got very hot, but the views were wonderful, right across the rolling country.

"Oo, I'm tired," said Ann. "When we get to the farm tonight, bags I not be cook."

"There isn't any farm tonight," said Mrs. Folds. "We're going to sleep under the stars. You can pretend you're pioneers opening up the Wild West."

"Oh, how gorgeous!" we chorused.

"But what are we going to *eat*?" howled April.

"Not to worry. We'll eat our emergency meal. You will be pleased to hear there'll be no cooking."

"But I've eaten mine!" cried April. "For snacks."

"Not all that food! You couldn't."

"I lost some of it."

"Now isn't that too bad?" said Rosevale. "You're going to be good and hungry by tomorrow morning."

April actually went pale, and Mercy said suddenly in a desperate voice, "I—I—I'm afraid I've lost mine too."

"We'll have to shoot some rabbits and skin them and roast them over the fire," said Rosevale, jogging cheerily along with dangling legs and her stirrup leathers crossed.

"But we haven't got any g—g—guns," said Mercy dolefully.

"Really?" said Rosevale. "Didn't you bring one? That was thoughtless of you."

"Oh, leave her alone, Rosevale," I said. "She believes everything you say."

By five o'clock Mrs. Folds had decided we'd ridden enough for one day. We had discovered a sheltered spot up on the moors, with grazing for the ponies and a clear, rushing stream, so after we had all had a rest, flat on our backs, she set us cutting heather for the beds with cutters produced from the stores carried by the pack pony. The ponies were examined and were all in tip-top condition and taking to the life of the wild, we agreed, like one o'clock.

"Which is more than I can say about me," said Ann. "Gosh, I am stiff. Got any embrocation in your first-aid, Jill?"

"Just pony stuff." I said. "I thought it would do for both."

"Well, it should. You can rub my back with it when we go to bed and I'll rub yours."

"It grows fur," said Diana. "I know a girl who used it and she turned into a bear."

"I don't believe you," said Mercy.

"There you are," said Rosevale. "That's something she doesn't believe. But it might take the skin off."

"Bosh!" said Ann. "I should think on the whole that my skin's tougher than George's."

We got out the sleeping-bags, and the food which we pooled. There was a beautiful collection, tinned meat, salmon, sardines, biscuits, cake, nuts and raisins, cheese and sweets. We drew water from the stream and made tea in a big billy-can, and then had a bathe in a deep pool which looked cool and tempting and proved to be like melted ice. Shrieks broke forth as we leapt in.

After that, what with the long day's riding and the food and the bathing, we were so tired that we couldn't say a word, hardly even good night. We struggled down into our sleeping-bags on our heather couches and fell fast asleep as dusk came stealing over the distant hills. The last thing I heard was the sound of the ponies cropping grass at the end of their tether ropes.

It was a thrilling thing to wake next morning and find yourself in the open and see a pink dawn come creeping over the hilltops, but while I was getting all rapturous some people were already moaning about what a night they'd had with their sunburn and their midge bites.

"I say," said Ann. "I wonder what's for breakfast?"

"What was left over from supper, I guess," said Rosevale. "All cold and bitty and nibbled by mice probably. We're pioneers, remember?"

By now everybody was rushing down to wash in the stream and nearly kicking me out of my sleeping-bag, and Ann was shouting, "Oh, come and look at Black Boy, Jill, he's done something to his leg."

I shot out in flapping pyjamas, expecting something terrible, but there was only a scratch you could hardly see, about half an inch long.

"You are a fusser," I said. "I'll slosh a bit of Dettol on just to make sure."

By the time we were dressed breakfast was ready, and Mrs. Folds had miraculously produced packets of corn flakes to say nothing of tins of condensed milk —the pack pony must have been finding things much lighter by now—and we made a fire and drank coffee and sat about in the heather making jokes.

"Aren't we lucky?" said Mrs. Folds. "It's going to be another lovely fine day."

The sun burst through the clouds and all the sheep in the world seemed suddenly to start bleating.

The Third Day

"WHEN you come to think of it," said Ann trotting along beside me, "nothing really happens, does it?"

"How do you mean, nothing happens?"

"Well, we just ride on and on."

"It's jolly nice."

"Yes, but when you go on a pony trek you expect out of the ordinary things to happen. You've read books about pony treks—I don't mean that Ecuador thing when there were snakes and all the perils of the jungle—but this sort of trek—and the people discover a spy lurking in the woods and chase him and hand him over to the police, or somebody falls over a cliff. Or sometimes they find a body and it turns out to be somebody famous, or they save somebody's life."

"That's just books," I said. "I think it's all a bit silly and kiddish."

April who was riding just ahead of us and trying to turn her head round and listen to what we were saying, suddenly came off her pony backwards and sat down on the track with a thud.

We waited for her to get up but she didn't.

"I've broken something," she said crossly. "I'm bleeding to death. It's running down me."

Wendy jumped down in great concern.

"Let me see, April—well, there isn't any blood that I can see. It looks like dirty water."

"Oh, oh, it's my fish!" cried April. "Catch it, quick."

She had caught a fish in the stream where we camped and was carrying it in a potted meat jar full of water tied on to her saddle. She started scrabbling about on the ground looking for it.

"What on earth—?" said Mrs. Folds. "What's happened?"

"April's lost her fish. The jar broke."

"I can't find it," said April, going red in the face. "It was a nice one with funny eyes. I was going to send it to the zoo."

"Look, if you're going to collect anything on this trip," said Mrs. Folds, "can't you stick to flowers, or even stones if you're geologically minded, but heavens above, not fish!"

"It was a special fish," said April. "I bet it was valuable. It was all your fault, Ann, talking about dead bodies that you'd found."

"I never did!" said Ann. "It was your fault for turning round to listen to Jill and me and not looking where you were going."

"Oh, get up April, and let's get on," said Wendy.

"You cruel beast!" said April. "What about my fish, it'll die if we don't find it."

"If this is it, it doesn't look too good," said Jackie, picking an obviously dead stickleback off her shoe. "And it's only a stickleback. Valuable my foot!"

April mounted and rode on, sulking.

"I'll catch you another, the next stream we come to," said Wendy kindly. "Let's play at something.

What about car registrations? The letters on my car are PCD. What do they stand for?"

"Please Come to Dinner," said Ann.

"Too many words."

"Plumbers Can't Dance," said Diana.

"Police Constable Dixon," said Jackie.

"That one wins," said Wendy. "Now it's your turn, Jackie."

"Oh, I can't think of anything—oh, yes, YTF."

"Gosh, how awful. Yellow-tailed Flamingo."

"You Three Flops," shouted Ann.

"Your Tyre's Flat," I suggested.

"That one wins," said Jackie. "Your turn, Jill."

While I was thinking April turned round and said sulkily, "MFD, and it means My Fish Died, and I call it a silly rotten game."

"Don't take any notice of Sourpuss," said Rosevale. "Go on, Jill."

"IAF," I said at random.

"Isn't April Fat," said Rosevale. "That's too easy."

"IHY," said April, "meaning I Hate You."

"Let's stop this," said Wendy. "It's too nice a day to fight."

Ahead of us the others had found a level stretch and broken into a gallop. We couldn't wait to dash after them, in a glorious, thrilling, pounding music of hoofs. And even April forgot all about her fish and her mood and was grinning with joy like everybody else.

We slowed down, panting, and gave the ponies a breather, and Mrs. Folds told us something about the history of the country we were riding through and about a battle that had been fought there in the Wars of the Roses, and about a coaching inn where a notorious highwayman used to make his headquarters.

77

In the afternoon we found ourselves riding down a long valley, and suddenly somebody shouted out, "Oh, look, the sea!"

(You will remember that some Greek with a name like furniture polish said the same thing in the Ancient History book.)

It really was the sea, a shimmering blue triangle at the bottom of the valley.

We bounced in our saddles. "Are we really going down to the sea? Is there a village? Can we stop there a bit? Can we paddle? Can we bathe? Can we stay there all night?"

Mrs. Folds said there was a very attractive village down there, and we could stay for a couple of hours and do what we liked—within reason—only first we had better stop by the roadside for a few minutes and tidy up, as some people she wouldn't name looked as if they'd just come out of the jungle, and after all this was where we had to show that we were respectable Pony Club members.

We dismounted on the grass verge, much to the ponies' joy as the grass looked particularly juicy, and everybody combed their hair and peeped into the corner of somebody's pocket glass, and took the smears off their faces with handkerchiefs, and pushed down their shirts and hitched up their slacks.

"We shall ride into the village slowly and carefully," said Mrs. Folds, "so as not to get mixed up with the odd things that wander about village streets. Single file, please, and well into the side. I lead and Wendy will bring up the rear. And no ragging or showing off!"

It was a lovely seaside village with pink and yellow cottages and red roofs, and it had a cobbled street which led down to a slipway and on to the shore.

Most of the inhabitants seemed to be outside their doors to have a good look at us, and they must have decided we were all right because they smiled and waved, and we smiled and waved back, and felt like King Arthur's knights arriving at Camelot or something equally dotty.

Mrs. Folds stopped and asked a man where we could park twelve ponies for about two hours, and he said he had a nice yard where they'd come to no harm, which on inspection proved to be true.

Then we all went off in a mob to see what we could find in the village. The first thing we did was to buy postcards to send home. The village had the intriguing name of Watloh-on-Tide, and there seemed to be five picture postcards available, High Tide at Watloh, Low Tide at Watloh, The Main Street from the Slipway, The Slipway from the Main Street, and a rather vague one called Sunset Waves which might have been anywhere.

It took ages to decide which one to have. In the end I bought High Tide to send to Mummy, and with one of my rare noble impulses I blued another fivepence on Sunset Waves for Miss Crombie. Then we all had to surge along to the small Post Office to buy stamps. We each bought one or two twopence-halfpenny ones.

Mrs. Folds said, "I suppose you realise you've been more than half an hour over that? I thought you wanted to get down to the sea."

When we explained how long it took ten people to buy about fifteen stamps she said, "I suppose it didn't occur to you that you could have reckoned up how many you wanted and let one person buy the lot?"

And of course it hadn't, and no wonder the girl at the Post Office had looked a bit dizzy.

Then Katy Smith said, "Please, Mrs. Folds, where can we go to write our postcards?"

"There's always the beach," said Mrs. Folds. "I thought that was what you wanted."

Diana said, "Please couldn't we just for once go to a café, because then we could write the postcards on the tables, and you couldn't actually call it having a meal if it was just ices and cakes?"

And Mrs. Folds said we could do exactly as we liked, but remember we only had two hours altogether and the time was going.

We charged off to see what the village had in the way of a café. Actually there were two, so we had to spend ages deciding between The Merry Teapot and Nibblers' Nook and finally piled into the latter as Wendy said the name was original and perhaps the cakes would be original too, but they weren't, they proved to be either the gooey kind or the pebbly kind.

So while we ate we wrote the postcards, and as there were only three ball-point pens among the party we had to borrow them in turns, and that took a lot of time.

When we emerged from the portals of Nibblers' Nook and had posted the cards we found to our horror that we had only half an hour of our two hours left and the shades of evening were practically falling. Those who had swimsuits wanted to bathe and the rest wanted to paddle, so it was one mad rush into the cooling waves, until Wendy rounded everybody up and pointed out that we still had five miles to ride to the farm where we were staying the night.

We hated coming out of the sea.

"Cheer up," Wendy said, "there'll be a lovely supper when we get to it. We've bought fish from the fishermen here, and we'll grill them and roast

potatoes, but you'd better hurry up or it'll be about midnight before we get it."

When we got back into our saddles we were so tired that we swayed about and nearly went to sleep, and Ann said she felt as if she was riding by remote control.

"We seem to do such a lot in a day," I said, looking anxiously at Mercy who was practically lying on her pony's neck, dead to the world.

"MERCY! WAKE UP!"

"Where am I?" murmured Mercy in the tones of the sleeping beauty.

Everybody began to giggle, but we had to pull ourselves up with a jerk as a three-ton lorry suddenly came charging down the lane. We only just had time to get the ponies collected and pressed into the hedge when it swept by, and some of them, quite terrified, began prancing and bucking.

Katy toppled into the road, and the rest of us slid down rather too quickly, grabbing at bridles.

"Gosh! He could have been a bit more careful," raged Diana. "Most drivers are decent when they're passing ponies, but that one was the very depths."

"Is everybody all right?" said Mrs. Folds, helping Katy up. "Are you all right, Katy?"

"Yes, I've only grazed my arm a bit, it's nothing."

We quieted the ponies down.

"That brute of a man!" said Wendy. "I bet he was in a hurry for no good purpose. Probably his lorry's full of stolen television sets."

"I got his number," said Rosevale. "It was 7972."

"What registration letters?"

"I didn't have time to get those."

We remounted rather soberly and rode on, very wide awake by now, and we were all glad when Mrs.

Folds said at last, "That's the farm we're making for. At last! There's a wood behind it where we're going to camp."

Jackie Heath gave a hollow groan.

"Me, I could do with a nice soft bed for once. My bones are all sticking out in bumps. If there's any choice, what about a loft with lots of hay like we had the first night?"

The farmer and his wife greeted us as if we were things from outer space. They just couldn't get the idea of people riding around the countryside on ponies for enjoyment. But they were kind people, and when we explained about the state of our bones, said that those who wanted could sleep in a nice hayloft with lots of cosy straw, and it was so tempting that several people said they would, in spite of the jeers of the tough ones who wanted to camp out of doors.

"Let's get the barbecue up before we do anything else," said April. "Honestly I'm starving to death. My front's touching my back."

"Right," said Wendy. "I'll see to the barbecue and you can start cleaning the fish."

"What!" howled April.

"Here you are." Wendy sloshed down a huge wet parcel. "Somebody's got to do it, so get cracking. The fire will be ready by the time the fish is. There's a basket of potatoes ready at the back door, so some of you people get them washed for roasting."

"No place for layabouts on a trek," I said sarkily.

"You're telling us!"

Everybody was kept busy, and of course Mrs. Folds insisted that the ponies should be attended to first. There was a nice field for them, and for the next half-hour I was unsaddling and staggering to the tack room while the farmer's children stood and watched with their mouths open.

"We can ride," one of them said. "We can ride bullocks. Bet you can't ride bullocks."

I felt like saying I'd try anything once, but I was too hungry and tired.

The other child said, "We had two calves stolen today."

"When?" I said.

"Just a bit before you came."

"Did you hear that?" I said to Ann who was helping me. "I wonder. It could have been that lorry. The driver behaved just like you'd expect a cattle thief to, didn't he?"

She said we might as well go and tell the farmer about our adventure with the charging lorry, and he was very interested.

The calves had been in a field by the roadside, out of sight of the house, and they had just disappeared.

"Sure, they must have been in that lorry," said Rosevale. "And the number was 7972 only I didn't get the letters."

"Ring up Archie," said the farmer's wife. "Tell him to come round."

Archie was the local policeman. He soon appeared on a motor-bike and seemed very surprised to see us. It was like being on television, telling him the story, and as we were all trying to tell him at once he nearly got his pencil tied in a knot.

"Go ahead, Jackie. Everybody else pipe down," said Mrs. Folds.

"He was tearing along the road like a mad thing," said Jackie. "He never even slowed down when he saw us, much less try to avoid us. If we hadn't been very quick and experienced riders, and got the ponies into the hedge, he'd have murdered half of us."

"And what about these calves?"

The farmer told the story, about the two calves being in the field by the roadside out of sight of the house, and how they'd just disappeared.

"Very suspicious circumstances," said Archie, finishing off his writing with a flourish. "I'll get back to the station and put in a few calls. 7972, you said but no letters available. Right!"

"Gosh," said Ann. "Isn't this dramatic."

"I don't want to be dramatic," April moaned. "Can't we get on with supper? It's awfully late, and I've been dying of hunger for hours, and I even cleaned the fish. It jolly well isn't fair."

We were ravenous, and the fish and potatoes were cooked to a turn and so good that we soon cheered up.

We washed everything up, and then Mrs. Folds said, why not have a concert? She was sure some of us could do something.

Rosevale said she could sing hill-billy songs if she had a guitar, but she hadn't, and they didn't sound right without one. Mercy said she could sing *John Peel*, so we started off with that and we all joined in the chorus. Mercy had a nice deep voice, which you wouldn't have expected, and we had a terrific time seeing who could hang on to the Halloo-oo-oos the longest.

Katy and Billie Smith sang a close harmony duet which was frightfully soppy, all about "so blue without yew", and the harmony kept coming unstuck, but the farmer's wife who was listening said they ought to be on the wireless because they were as good as any sister act she'd ever heard.

Then Ann and I did our dialogue out of *Viceroy Sarah* that we did at the end of term concert at school—Ann was the Duchess and I was Queen Anne —and Diana, who thought she was the coming Dorothy Tutin, recited yards of Ophelia and Desdemona, and by then I think Mrs. Folds wished she hadn't suggested the concert. So we all finished up by singing *The Yellow Rose of Texas*, and just as we were singing it for the fourth time the telephone started ringing in the house.

"I wouldn't be surprised if that's Archie," said the farmer's wife. "I wonder if they've got on to anything?" She ran up to the house, and we all followed in a flock, and met the farmer coming out.

"They've got the lorry," he said. "Stopped it sixty miles away. Pretty hot, the police. It was the goods all right, but my calves weren't in it. It was full of stolen television sets."

"That's what Wendy said," gasped Ann.

"Golly!" said Wendy. "I must have got X-ray eyes."

"Could you really see inside?" said Mercy simply, and we all shrieked with laughing.

"It serves that man right," said Diana. "Now they'll put him in prison, and if he'd been decent and courteous to us we'd never have noticed him and he'd have got away with it."

"That's what's called poetic justice," said Mrs. Folds.

"But what about my calves?" said the farmer. "I suppose the young lady couldn't be psychic about them?"

"Well, my father is a farmer," said Wendy, "and I did just wonder whether some children might have let them out of the field to play with. That happened to some calves of ours once, and they wandered for miles."

"Could be!" said the farmer. "I never thought of that. The local children wouldn't do such a fool thing, but I did hear that Mrs. Price had got some town children staying with her. I think I'll slip round there."

To make a long story short, Wendy was right. The children who were staying with Mrs. Price came from London, and seeing the calves in the field they had gone inside to play with them and then run off home to tea without shutting the gate. The calves were discovered on a common about three miles away, and of course they might have been killed on the road when darkness fell and perhaps wrecked a car too.

"If town children come to stay in the country, they ought to be taught to respect country ways," said the farmer. "Shutting gates, or better still not opening them, and not walking through fields of crops or standing hay, and leaving animals alone. That's what Mrs. Price ought to have told them, and I'll go along tomorrow and give her a piece of my mind." He stared at Wendy and said, "She must have got second sight, she must!"

The Fourth Day

BEING one of the tough ones who had chosen to sleep outside under the stars, I lay in my sleeping-bag and thought how pretty the sky looked, like a black spangled veil caught up by the moon like a brooch. With such beautiful ideas in my mind I fell asleep, and woke gasping as somebody began to throw water over me.

"Stop it!" I yelled. "You beast!"

"Get up quick," said a voice. "It's pouring."

The rain was streaming down from a dark grey sky, and the next minute we were a struggling shouting mass of people, jumping out of our sleeping-bags and hopping around as the rain soaked our pyjamas.

"The barn—quick!" shouted somebody.

We charged along in bare feet through the sopping grass, and painfully found the hard cobbles of the yard. April fell flat on her face, Billie tripped over her dangling sleeping-bag and fell clonk on top of April, I tried to drag them up and turned a somersault myself. We couldn't see for the wet hair falling over our faces, but at last we burst into the barn like a herd of maddened rhinos.

There wasn't a sound in there but gentle snoring.

Our comrades were slumbering peacefully above in the loft. Then a faint voice muttered, "What's the matter down there?"

"It's us!" shouted Rosevale. "There's a flood. We're washed out."

"Brrrrr!" said Ann. "I'm freezing."

By now the people at the farm were about and had realised what was happening. The farmer's wife ran out with a mack over her head and cried, "Come along in the kitchen, there's a big fire, and bring some towels."

Fortunately our towels and clothes were all in the barn, and soon we were dried down and dressed.

"Now for the ponies," said Wendy. "They'll be in a horrid mess."

"You can take them into the big shed and rub them down," said the farmer, "and the man will make them a hot mash."

Several of us pulled on our macks and rushed away to see to this. The poor ponies were standing miserably huddled under a tree, and were glad to be rescued. Soon we had them inside, and the farmer's man helped us to rub them down while the rest of our party prepared breakfast.

"You'd better bring that breakfast in here," said the farmer's wife kindly, as she bustled to make room for us in the big kitchen.

"There are times when the outdoor life comes unstuck," Mrs. Folds said laughing. "It's most kind of you to put up with such an invasion."

"Mummy, are they all going to live here always?" asked the little boy, and we all laughed.

The table was laid and soon we were sitting down to porridge, bacon and tea round the enormous table.

"Do you think it's going to clear?" Mrs. Folds

asked the farmer anxiously as we peered through the streaming windows.

"Not this morning it isn't. It might improve this afternoon. You can't think of setting off while it's like this."

We washed up and then retired to the loft to have a council of war while the rain drummed and swished outside.

"I know! We'll have a pony quiz," said Mrs. Folds. "It'll do our brains good."

"Oh, it'll be worse than school," April groaned.

"We'll have a panel of four, and fire questions at them," said Mrs. Folds. "Let me see . . . Wendy can be on the panel to start with—and Jill—and Billie—and Mercy."

"Oh, please, not me!" implored Mercy looking as if she had just been condemned to death. "I don't know a thing, truly I don't."

"Then you ought to," said Wendy callously. "None of us feel very bright if it comes to that."

"But you're clever and I haven't got any brains at all."

"Gosh," I said, "you look as if you were climbing up the steps of the guillotine."

We four sat in a row and the others ganged up in front of us.

"Don't make the questions too tough," said Billie.

"I can't think of any questions at all," said Ann.

"Okay, I'll start," said Mrs. Folds. "Wendy, what is a Grade C competition?"

"Where the fences are under four feet," said Wendy. She made a face, fanned herself with her hand, and said "Whew!"

"There's a little more to it than that, but it'll pass for a start. Now, Ann, you ask Jill something."

"I could ask Jill a lot," Ann said giving me an old-fashioned look, "but I think—well, what's the first thing you'd look for in a good horse?"

"A nice honest eye," I said promptly, "and I know where you got that one from."

She had got it from the last pony book we had read, called *Riding With Gusto,* in which there was an ancient stableman who was always saying, "What I looks for in a hoss is a nice honest eye."

"Let me ask Billie one," said April. "What's navicular disease?"

"What's what?" said Billie.

"Navicular disease."

"Oh, *help!*" said Billie disgustedly.

"I don't suppose anybody but me knows," said April.

"Go on, then, what is it?" said Wendy.

"It's what a pony gets from trotting too fast on hard roads," said April, and we all groaned.

"I'm sure none of you are likely to trot a pony too fast on hard roads," said Mrs. Folds, "so you're not likely to come up against that complaint. Diana, you can ask Mercy a question."

I could see Diana's eyes glinting wickedly while poor Mercy went paler and paler as she squirmed, waiting.

"What's a canaletti?" said Diana.

"Look," Mrs. Folds interrupted, "can we have less of these fancy questions? A canaletti is a small pole jump, so let's call it a small pole jump and have done with it. Diana, please ask a more reasonable question, and Mercy, stop looking as if a bomb was going to drop on you."

"Here's one," said Diana. "How would you calm a pony that was bashing about in a horse box?"

"G-g-g-give him some sugar?" said Mercy feebly.

"Can anybody else on the panel answer that?" said Mrs. Folds.

"Take him out and walk him up and down," I said.

"Right. Question for Wendy, please."

"Why do we have to clean the tack every night?" Rosevale asked.

"Because if you don't it goes stiff and galls the pony. That's easy."

"I've got one for Jill," said April. "Why did she say I had a weak seat, that time I fell off?"

"Because your legs were too far back," I said. "Your centre of gravity was therefore wrong. It always is if your legs——"

"Oh, get lost!" said April. "It's always legs. Jill's got leg mania."

"Legs are the most important thing in riding," said Jackie Heath.

"I'm sick of hearing about them," said April. "So what?"

"It's my turn," said Katy. "I've thought of one. Why in competitions do I jump the difficult fences well and mess up the simple ones?"

"Who's the question for?"

"Mercy."

"Oh, *no!*" wailed Mercy.

"Go ahead, chump," said Wendy.

"I sh-sh-sh-should th-th-th-thing—I mean, you probably trust to luck when you walk the course instead of studying the difficulties. I simply never do anything but look for the difficulties," she ended sadly.

Everybody roared with laughing, but Mrs. Folds said, "You're absolutely right, Mercy. I couldn't have given a better answer myself. But, Mercy, I hope it isn't true that you do *nothing* but look for the difficulties, because a negative attitude in competitions is hopeless and means you'll never win. Don't ever be afraid to tell yourself that the jumps are just right for you, if you think they are. Confidence is everything in your favour, if it's genuine."

Mercy looked as if she doubted that any jumps on earth could be right for her, but Jackie said, "April, doesn't your father make you place your legs correctly?"

"Oh, sure," said April airily. "But it's so uncomfortable I just change it the minute he's gone."

"You're hopeless," said Jackie. "Absolutely gone."

We all felt a bit hopeless too, sitting answering pony questions in a loft with the rain thumping and squelching outside, when we ought to have been trekking in the sunshine.

Suddenly somebody shouted, "The sun's coming out! Look, you can see it sort of gleaming behind the clouds."

It was true. Everything changed as quickly as a pantomime scene. In half an hour the sky was clear blue and everything began to sparkle under the bright warm sun. We rushed around, saddling up and getting ready for off, and making scornful remarks to April who said, wouldn't it be a good idea to have lunch before we started?

We said good-bye and thank you very much for being so kind, to the people at the farm, and trotted off merrily towards the woods which lay in the distance. Soon we were riding along a broad grassy track with spreading woods on each side.

"We can canter for quite a distance here," said Mrs. Folds. "Not too fast, please. And if anybody feels they're lagging behind, just shout out."

The woods were fascinating and looked as though

nobody ever went there. Fallen trees had been left to lie until they were covered with green moss, and the undergrowth was choked with creepers and ground ivy. It was so silent that you could imagine crowds of little animals and birds nervously watching us, unseen, and wondering what we were up to.

Soon the track turned downhill and became slippery. Brambles whipped across the path, people lost their caps and got scratched faces, and the ponies didn't like it a bit and became difficult to hold.

"Next thing, we'll get bogged down," said Ann, but we didn't. The track began to open out and the woods thinned, and we could see that we were coming to a wide common. This was the outlet of the woods, marked by a huge fallen tree trunk which we all jumped with whoops of joy.

We were terribly hot and tired with hanging on to the restless ponies, so we decided this was the time for lunch. Out came the parcels which the farmer's wife had packed for us, revealing Cornish pasties, cheese, bread and cakes and biscuits. It tasted wonderful, and when we had finished we tidied up and wiped each other's bramble scratches, because we looked as if we had been fighting Red Indians.

"Oh, blow, my stirrup leather's nearly through," said Ann. "It's the stitching."

Mrs. Folds said we should soon be coming to a sizeable village where Ann could probably get it stitched. When we arrived there we found plenty of shops in the one street, and among them a saddler's where the man said he could repair the leather in about half an hour.

"There's no point in everybody waiting," said Mrs. Folds. "All you people and ponies will only cause a

traffic problem. We'll ride on, and Ann and Jill can follow."

"Which way?" I asked.

"We're making for Stedmoor, you can't go wrong."

They all went off, and we asked the village policeman where we could put the ponies. He showed us an inn yard where we could tie them, after which we wandered about the village and looked at the shops and bought some sweets and ice-cream tubs.

"It's half an hour," said Ann. "Let's go back to the saddler's."

He kept us waiting for about another half-hour, but at last the leather was ready, Ann paid for it, and we went to collect our ponies.

"The others will be riding slowly, I expect," I said. "If the road's good and there's a grass verge we ought to catch them up fairly soon."

A quarter of a mile beyond the village we came to a four-way cross-roads.

"Where now?" said Ann.

I just sat and opened my mouth.

"Where are we making for?" said Ann.

Realisation flooded me with icy shocks, as it says in books.

"I can't remember," I said. "Didn't you hear what Mrs. Folds said?"

"I wasn't taking any notice," Ann said. "You *must* remember!"

"But I don't. It just didn't sink in."

"Well, I'll read out the names on all the signposts and you'll recognise the one."

She read out all the places, but they didn't seem to mean a thing. We sat and stared at each other.

"Now we've had it!" Ann said.

"No we haven't," I said optimistically. "Let's take

the most country-looking road. That's sure to be the one." And I set off blithely up the road I had chosen. Ann hesitated for a minute and then followed me, saying, "You said it—not me!"

Actually I could have kicked myself, because it wasn't so much a case of forgetting the name of the place but I hadn't even paid enough attention to notice it, so that when Ann read out the names on the signpost not one of them meant a thing to me.

"We might come across their hoof marks soon," said Ann hopefully.

We didn't, but that didn't necessarily mean anything. After a mile or so the road began to wind sharply upwards and came out on a wide stretch of open moorland which extended for miles. We gazed into the distance, hoping to see ponies, but there was nothing. The grass verges were wide, so we cantered, still hoping. The whole landscape seemed deserted, it was a very lonely road. I thought, We're sure to come to some place soon. Somebody might have seen the others. But already I had a chilly feeling that I'd chosen the wrong road.

We'd ridden seven or eight miles by now. There wasn't any point in going back.

At last we came to a tiny moorland hamlet where we were definitely told that no ponies and riders had passed through.

"I'm frightfully sorry," I said to Ann. "It's all my fault. I was an absolute dope."

"That's okay," she said. "We're lost. So what?"

"If we went back to the place where we got the leather stitched," I said, "we wouldn't be any better off, and if we go on there's nothing to stop us ending up in Scotland."

"The others will wait and wait for us," said Ann.

"They won't be able to imagine why we don't turn up."

"We'd better go on," I said. "We may get to a bigger village than this and find somebody who can suggest something. How much money have you go?"

"About twelve shillings."

"I've got less than that. We shall have to dial 999."

"What are you talking about?"

"It's an emergency, isn't it? I've always wanted to."

"We'll look fine," said Ann, "if about six fire engines come roaring up. Anyway, there isn't a telephone in this place."

The ponies trudged on, and the road became a zigzag lane leading right into desolation. Hot, tired and hungry we dismounted and gazed at the unfriendly hills around. It was half-past six. No tea, no shelter, no nothing. Golly! I thought. You can keep the great open spaces and the roving life.

The Fifth Day

IT wasn't a bit funny. Just put yourself in our place.

"Look!" I said suddenly. "There's a house!"

"Where? I can't see it."

"Against the hillside. And it's got a telephone! Come on."

It was the loneliest house you ever saw, miles from anywhere, and standing back one field's width from the road.

We turned the ponies into the cart track which led up to it.

"I say, do you think we ought?" said Ann. "It looks sort of grue and sinister to me. It's probably the headquarters of a gang of international smugglers. They'll gag and bind us."

"We can talk our way out of it," I said. "All I want is to get at their phone. If they gag and bind us we can crawl across to the phone and knock the receiver off with our heads and tap Morse into it with our noses like Inspector Charlesworth."

"I still think it's grue," said Ann.

"Oh, come on. Don't be awkward."

We rode up to the house which was silent and apparently quite deserted. There were some outbuildings at the side, but nothing alive except a few hens and ducks.

We knocked at the door and waited, and knocked again and waited a long time. Dead silence.

"That's that," said Ann. "Nobody home."

"I'm going to have one more bash," I said, and fairly thundered on the door.

"Wait, I can hear something," said Ann who had ears like a hare. "I can! Listen—gosh, it's like somebody saying help, very faint."

I could hear it too. I pushed open the letter box and peeped through. I could see a hall and a flight of stairs, and a woman lying on the floor at the bottom of the stairs. I could see her face, and she was muttering Help!

"How can we get in?" I shouted.

"Open the door. It isn't locked."

We rushed in. She looked all tangled up and she didn't move.

"Did you fall downstairs?" said Ann.

"Yes. I tripped. I've broken my leg. I can't move at all or I'd have crawled to the phone. My husband's away till tomorrow. Oh, I can't believe somebody has really come at last. Hardly anybody comes here."

"We mustn't move her," said Ann, who was very hot on first-aid. "I'll dash upstairs and find a pillow and some blankets to put over her, and you can go and ring up your old 999, Jill."

"Say it's Mrs. Cole at Underlock House," said the woman. "The operator knows me."

I was excited. At last one of my wildest dreams was going to be fulfilled, to ring 999.

I picked up the telephone and the minute the operator answered I said, "Nine-nine-nine—as quick as you can," in a sort of M.I.5 voice.

"Who are you, and what do you want?" said the operator, which wasn't the way it should have gone at all.

"I want Emergency," I said, with a dark bark.

"Where are you speaking from?" asked the operator who simply wouldn't play it like the books. "What's the matter, anyway?"

"If this was television," I said, "the worst would have happened by now. Listen, Mrs. Cole of Underlock House has fallen downstairs and broken her leg and a few other things, and we've lost nine people and ten ponies, and you're not doing a thing about it."

"Good gracious! Mrs. Cole! What happened? Where's Mr. Cole? What happened to the horses?"

"Just get on with that 999!" I yelled.

"Well, what do you want? Ambulance, Fire, or Police?"

"The lot!" I shouted. "And tell them to hurry!"

"Oh, dear. I'll see what I can do."

Ann was making a cup of tea for Mrs. Cole, who must have been feeling frightful but was very brave and so glad that she wasn't going to be left lying there for hours and hours until Mr. Cole came home tomorrow.

While we were waiting we told her about ourselves and about the trek and getting lost.

"So, you see, even if we have saved you, Mrs. Cole, you've saved us too, because you gave us a change to ring 999, and now they'll have to find our party for us."

About half an hour later a car came dashing up to the door. It was a police car, and out jumped an Inspector and a constable and a man carrying a doctor's bag.

He was the first into the house. He said, "Where's

Mrs. Cole? What's happened to her?" Then he saw her lying on the floor at the bottom of the stairs with the pillow and the blankets, and said, "Thank goodness, somebody's had the sense not to try to move her."

"I learnt it at first-aid," said Ann looking smug.

The doctor knelt down beside Mrs. Cole, and the Inspector said to me, "You come along in here," and led the way into the kitchen.

"Now then," he said, "what's all this about? Something about a fire or a flood that's done for a lot of people and horses? Calling out the fire engine, and I don't know what!"

"It's that telephone operator," I said. "She didn't get with it at all. My friend and I were lost——"

I patiently began at the beginning and told him the whole story, and added that it was a jolly good thing we'd called at Underlock House or poor Mrs. Cole would have been dead.

"So you just asked for 999, did you?"

"Naturally," I said. "And I'm glad you came and brought the doctor, and now that Mrs. Cole is all right, would you mind putting out a 'Calling All Cars' because our party will be stuck somewhere waiting for us, and we've got to get there somehow."

The Inspector said, "You ought to be in Dixon of Dock Green, that's where you ought to be. But I don't doubt that we can locate your party for you if you'll give us a little time. I'm glad it's nothing worse. I expected to find flames a mile high, or the Battle of Waterloo, or something."

The doctor then put his head inside the door and said. "I'm not going to wait for an ambulance, it'll take an hour to get here. We can put Mrs. Cole on the back seat of the car and run her to the hospital."

While they were settling her comfortably in the car, Mrs. Cole kept on thanking us over and over again, and we said we hoped she would soon be better, and really we were very grateful to her because actually it was her accident that got us out of our fix, not that we were glad about her broken leg but she'd understand what we meant.

She said, "It's getting late, so if it suits you just spend the night here. There's a bed made up in the room with the blue carpet, and there's plenty of food. Help yourselves, and perhaps you wouldn't mind feeding the livestock?"

Meanwhile the Inspector had been telephoning, and now he came out and said, "We'll soon have your party traced, and I'll ring you here when I get some news."

Then the Inspector, the constable, and the doctor all packed into the front of the car with Mrs. Cole in the back, and they drove away.

"Isn't life comic?" said Ann. "About an hour ago we were lost in the wilds and starving to death, and now we've got a house and food and a bedroom with a blue carpet and some hens. She said we could eat, so let's. I'll bang up some food while you see to the ponies. Christmas, we've forgotten them!"

Black Boy and George were wandering aimlessly round the outside of the house. I found a field for them and they trotted happily in and made for the shade of a chestnut tree where the grass looked lush and green. In the kitchen Ann was scrambling eggs at the calor-gas cooker and on the table was a crusty cottage loaf, a dish of butter, an apple pie and a fruit cake. We found a tin of cocoa and plenty of milk and brewed up.

"This is marvellous," I said, as my famished inside
104

got the glad news of reinforcements. "I'm going to write a book called *It Pays to Get Lost*."

Ann said we were a bit selfish to feed ourselves before we fed the starving hens and ducks, but on the other hand it was no good starting to feed them and falling down dead with hunger while we did so.

I said she could wash up and leave the poultry to me, I was used to it and it would be just like home. I soon found the grain, and they all came flocking round me as if I was their long lost aunt.

Then three cats turned up, mewing and wrapping themselves round my legs. I guessed there must be some food for them somewhere, so I rummaged about and discovered some tins of Happi-Puss and a dish for milk.

"Hadn't you better look and see if there's anything in any of the sheds?" said Ann, and she must have been psychic because in a basket in one of the outhouses we found a pretty collie with three lovely pups. We found food for them too, and sat playing with the puppies for ages. They were wonderful, and crawled all over us biting our hair and giving funny little growls.

Suddenly I heard the telephone ringing in the house and ran to answer it. It was the Inspector.

"We've located your party," he said cheerfully. "So you see we're more use than you think. They're at a place called Stedmoor, camping in the grounds of a big house. It's twelve miles away, so your leader says you're to stay where you are tonight and join them tomorrow, and start early. If you follow the road another mile you'll see a signpost with Stedmoor on it. You can't go wrong. Ask for the Hall. And she says she told you Stedmoor and she doesn't know how you managed to forget it."

"Oh, dear, I'm in for it!" I said. "But thank you very much for helping."

"It's all part of the service," he said. "So long. Sleep well."

I went and told Ann and she said that we'd never live it down, the others would slay us.

"Come on," I said, "let's go and find that bedroom with the blue carpet. I'm dropping."

But peace was not destined to be ours. The news had spread, like it does in the country however remote, and all Mrs. Cole's friends and relations started ringing up. We retold the story until our throats were sore.

"Let's not answer it any more," said Ann. "Let it ring."

"But it never stops ringing. It's going on all night. There it goes again! It's your turn. Tell whoever it is that the house has just been burnt to the ground and you're a famous film star."

Ann giggled, and when she came back from the phone she said, "That was Mr. Cole. He says he'll be home early in the morning so we're just to go when we're ready and leave everything as it is. And I had a brain wave, I told the operator not to put any more calls through. So now we can go to bed."

But Fate had not finished with us yet. We had got half-way up the stairs when the front door bell rang, and then without waiting the letter box was pushed open and a voice said, "It's only me, Mrs. Appleyard."

I went and opened the door and Mrs. Appleyard came in. She was very large and had on odd shoes, which she hadn't noticed.

"I'm the next door neighbour," she said, "if you can call it next door, being a mile away. As soon as

I'd given the men their supper I just rushed round. You poor little things!"

We blinked because we didn't feel at all like poor little things.

"You can't possibly stay here all alone all night," said Mrs. Appleyard, who had a rich wheezy voice. "It's unthinkable."

"But we're quite all right," said Ann. "We've had a good supper and we're just going up to bed."

"As if I'd let you!" said Mrs. Appleyard. "Two little girls all alone. I'm going to stay with you. I've come all ready. I've brought my nightie and my little alarm clock." And she waved a string shopping bag at us.

We went cold all over. Did Mrs. Appleyard intend to tuck herself into bed with us?

"It's nearly ten now," I said feebly, "and we've decided to get up at five because we've got a long ride. It's hardly worth going to bed at all."

"Oh, yes, it is, dear. Now come along upstairs and we'll see what we can find. I'll set my alarm clock for five, and then I'll get up and make you a beautiful breakfast for being so kind to poor Mrs. Cole. It's the least I can do."

With sinking hearts we followed Mrs. Appleyard upstairs, dreading what we should find. I was ready to suggest that she should have the room with the blue carpet and we would park ourselves on the sofa downstairs. But fortunately her intentions were not the worst.

"I'm going to pop myself into Mrs. Cole's bed," she said. "I know she won't mind. And it'll make me feel so happy to think that I'm looking after you two."

She fussily wound up her alarm clock.

"I like to be right to the tick," she said. She then insisted on pulling our bed down to see if it was damp, and of course it wasn't, but that didn't satisfy Mrs. Appleyard. Down she went to the kitchen where she dug out a stone hot water bottle which looked as if it had come out of the ark, and we had to stand by while she boiled a kettle and filled it. Then up we trailed again, carrying this monster between us.

"You must leave your bedroom door open, and I'll leave mine open, and you'll feel you have company," she boomed.

By now we were nearly choking, trying not to laugh, and at last we got into bed, Mrs. Appleyard keeping up a running commentary all the time from her room to ours.

Our bed was huge and soft, having a feather mattress, and we sank down into a deep warm tunnel with that awful stone hot water bottle. Gently we put it out and lowered it on to the floor.

"Nightie-night!" called out Mrs. Appleyard at last. "I'll call you at half-past five when your brekky is ready."

"Nightie-night!" we sang back and then smothered our giggles in the pillows. In three minutes we heard gentle snores coming from Mrs. Appleyard, and I got up and softly shut her bedroom door, and ours. Then I flopped back into our bed, and we both banged our heads on the pillow five times to make us wake up at five o'clock. I don't know if you ever do this, but it works. We slept like little chicks in a nest, and when I woke it was five minutes to five and the sun was shining outside. A minute later Ann opened her eyes. We felt wonderful. We hopped out on to the blue carpet and dressed in silent haste.

From Mrs. Appleyard's room came strong, deep snores which sounded as if they would go on for ever.

It was five-fifteen. Either her famous alarm clock hadn't gone off, or nobody had noticed it.

We collected our things and crept downstairs to the kitchen. We made tea and had some bread and butter and marmalade, and washed up. I listened at the bottom of the stairs. Mrs. Appleyard snored on.

We were ready for off. It was six o'clock.

"Do you think we ought to wake her and tell her we're going?" said Ann.

I giggled. "If we do she'll never let us get away. She'll try and come with us, riding pillion behind you. It would be better if we were miles away when she wakes up."

I wrote on a piece of paper. "We are just going. Thank you very much. Don't forget the poultry and there are three cats and a dog and some puppies in the shed."

Then we shouldered the ponies' tack which we had piled in the hall, and stole silently out like the Arabs in the poem, and saddled up in the field, and we were away. I gave one last look back at Underlock House, half expecting to see Mrs. Appleyard's large astonished face at her bedroom window, but no.

"Whew!" said Ann. "We can't say that nothing ever happens to us. That was quite an adventure. And I adored those collie pups."

"It's funny," I said. "We do have adventures, but they're such homely sort of ones. I mean, we never get mixed up with Interpol, or see ghost riders, or anything like that. People in books do."

We came to a signpost.

"Wouldn't it be funny," Ann said, "if we'd forgotten the name of that place again?"

For a minute I went cold. I couldn't think.

"Stedmoor!" said Ann. "That's it. Twelve miles."

The Sixth Day

IN the park-like grounds of a big house we were reunited with the others. They were in a camp with real tents and equipment. All this belonged to some friends of Mrs. Folds, who lived at the house, and it had been previously arranged that the trek should end up there.

"Well, well, look who's here!" shouted April, bursting out of one of the tents in too tight jodpurs and a bitten apple in her hand. "You absolute squares not to remember where you were supposed to be going."

"Who's talking?" I said. "The squarest square that ever fell off a pony backwards."

Wendy appeared and cried, "Where did you finally get to? Did you have anything to eat? We pictured you sleeping in a haystack."

"You pictured wrong," said Ann. "We slept in a lovely feather bed with a hot water bottle, and we had heaps of food."

The others all flocked round us and didn't rag us at all. They were too interested in our adventures which we told at great length.

Mrs. Folds said, "I suppose I ought to be mad at you, but somehow I can't. Really, Jilly, I never knew anybody like you for falling on your feet. When other

110

people would be landed in an absolute mess, you find yourself a house and plenty to eat."

I told them about Mrs. Appleyard and they all shrieked.

"I expect she's still asleep," said Diana. "When she wakes up she won't know whether it's Wednesday or midnight in Moscow."

"At this minute," said Jackie, "she's probably creeping downstairs on tiptoe so as not to wake you, and when she's got your breakfast ready she'll call out wakey, wa-a-a-key!"

When we had stopped laughing I said, "What a wonderful place this is."

All around the camp spread the sunny parkland filled with grass and trees. The ponies were grazing, and everybody seemed to be extremely busy, in fact five people were sitting on the ground polishing saddles which seemed unusual.

"What's happened while we've been away?" we asked.

"For one thing," said Wendy, "those photographs we had taken at the inn on the first day have caught us up. Only they've got the titles mixed, it's rather a scream."

She went into the tent and came out with a newspaper called *The Poppledown Advertiser*, and on the front page was a photograph of us all with the ponies outside the inn, and also a photograph of a bunch of seaside donkeys.

The photographs themselves were quite good, only somebody had got the captions mixed, and under the donkeys it said, "Happy girls on trek", and under *us* it said, "You will meet these little beasts on the beach".

Of course we hooted with laughter, and just then

Mrs. Folds appeared and said, "Has anybody told you the news?"

"What news?"

"Well, the people who own this house and park are friends of mine. I arranged with them beforehand that we should finish up the trek here, and this afternoon there are going to be jumping competitions and we've been asked to enter and help the local cause along. That's going to be fun for you all. We're going to have lunch early—all laid on by the house—so go and rummage out your jodhs and clean shirts, I hope you've got some, and start cleaning your tack. The competitions don't start till four, so your ponies will get a good rest after their hack."

"Murder!" I said, clutching wildly at my hair. "What about a bit of practice?"

Wendy said, "Your ponies won't be too fresh, but that's your fault. There are practice jumps just behind the house—over there—and you can try them when you like."

"Double murder!" shrieked Ann. "We've got the ponies to groom and they're in a mess as they didn't get done yesterday, and our riding things must be creased, and what my clean shirt's like I can't think."

"Okay, okay," said Wendy. "Don't hit the roof. Mercy and Rosevale are up at the house now, pressing away like mad. If you take your jodhs and shirts up now I'm sure they'll do them for you."

"I'll groom your pony for ten bob, Jill," piped up April.

"Thanks," I said sarkily. "The poor thing's suffered enough. I'm going to have a go at him now and give him a last minute polish later. Come on, Ann, we'll have to get cracking."

"If you go up to the house they'll give you hot

water and everything you want. Absolutely everything's laid on here, it's sumptuous."

"And I hope your jumping's going to be
sumptuous," laughed Mrs. Folds. "I'm counting on
you not to let my reputation down."

You can guess how we all worked for the next few
hours. It was most exciting to see the white-railed
ring in the park, and we were all madly looking
forward to the competitions, except Mercy who said
she was sure she would do something awful and get
disqualified, and Jackie Heath who grumbled that she
couldn't be expected to do herself justice on a slug
like Marmion, and if only she'd had London Pride!

"I wonder what the opposition's going to be like?"
asked Katy Smith.

Mrs. Folds said that the other people would be
from the local Pony Club which was small but probably quite efficient.

"I hope we shan't go down to local history as the
flops from outer space," said Rosevale.

Diana said, not to worry, the locals couldn't be as
hot as all that, and she knew all about under-rating
the opposition, but it was even worse to under-rate
yourself, and that was a very different thing from getting big ideas about yourself, and we all clapped and
said, "Here endeth the pep-talk."

"You're just due to get one from me!" said Mrs.
Folds. "When you're ready I'm going to watch you
all do a round of the practice jumps, and make my
comments. Very frank comments, too, no bouquets."
She went on, "I've had a glimpse of some of you
already when you didn't know I was looking." (Hollow groans.) "April, you'll gain nothing by tearing
round the jumps at an unbalanced pace. It doesn't
even look good. Katy, there is such a thing as having

your legs too far forward where you can't use them efficiently. Mercy, I know you're tall, but do you have to look as if you were frightened your feet were going to brush the ground? They won't, you know. Diana, take up your stirrups another hole. And now come along."

We each did the four practice jumps under her eagle eye.

I nervously organised my forward seat and rode at the first pole jump. Black Boy pretended he didn't like the look of it, but tucked his feet in with exaggerated care and cleared it by inches. He also did the others without mishap and I heaved a sigh of relief but hoped he was not starting the day too well.

Ann followed me on George who behaved nicely, except that he never could resist a succulent hedge and stopped to take a mouthful.

"I expect I'll get told off for pulling and kicking," said April. "I always do, and I can't get round without, and that's that."

"If you've got to do it," I said, "do it invisibly. You honestly oughtn't to have to, April. If your pony knows the aids, why can't you apply them quietly?"

"I'll have a try," said April, and off she went to bounce around as usual.

"It's a good thing that pony's strong and patient," said Wendy. "I can see three counties through April's legs when she's above the jump."

Diana said it looked smart to stand up in your stirrups, and Martino Cassi always did it at Harringay, and we told her that if she thought she looked anything like Martino Cassi she had another think coming.

Billie Smith's pony was in a refusing mood and we were sorry for her. He wouldn't budge when he got to the gate jump, and as a last resort she gave him a slight swish with her stick whereupon he leapt straight into a cat jump and there was Billie hanging under his tummy.

Somebody picked her off and she started to weep.

"I'm not going to enter," she said. "It'll be awful this afternoon."

"Oh, be a sport," said Katy. "Everybody has their off days, and Piper will probably jump like an angel this afternoon. He's a show-off and won't do his best unless there's a real judge watching and crowds of people."

"Katy's right," said Mrs. Folds. "Just give Piper a piece of sugar, Billie—here's one—and let him watch the others."

Rosevale did a dramatic round, very circus-like, all flying hoofs and tightened reins and lying along the pony's neck.

"Very pretty," said Mrs. Folds drily. "Only you're not in the Laramie programme just now. And don't hold the mane. Country judges won't be impressed."

"Gosh, Rosevale, your pony's got hoofs like saucepan lids," shouted April. "If he did touch a jump it'd collapse in ruins."

"I want you all to remember," said Mrs. Folds, "to inspect the actual jumping course with the greatest of attention. Some of you may have been accustomed to a simple course with so many trotting strides between the jumps, but here for all we know the jumps may be set at awkward distances. It's up to you to look out for this, so that you're in a position to keep your pony going around at a balanced pace, not in a series of rushes and hesitations. Some of your ponies have the trick of cat jumping but that's neither graceful nor a good thing to rely on, even if it's useful

115

in an emergency. I like to see people ride with easy confidence."

"Easy confidence!" moaned Mercy. "Oh, dear. That's what I'll never have."

"Half the battle, Mercy, is to look as if you had it," said Mrs. Folds. "Keep your head up, all the time, and look relaxed."

"But I just look like a bunched up spider," wailed Mercy. "It's my legs and arms. I can't put pleats in them."

"Now that's enough misery!" said Mrs. Folds briskly. "You all know what you ought to do, and I'm relying on you to do it."

"And I'm quite sure they will," broke in an impressive voice, which came from Mrs. Gilpin whose house and park it was, and who had just walked in among us.

I thought she looked terrific. Although quite ancient—she could have been even fifty—her clothes were smashing. She had on beige corded slacks that really fitted and a supersonic emerald green sweater and a purple hair rinse that sort of backed up the sweater, if you know what I mean, and she had heaps of go in her and was obviously still able to enjoy herself in spite of her burden of years.

We all stared at her in admiration, and Wendy muttered to me, "I dare you to ask her what her lipstick is. Gosh, I'd like one like it."

"Ask her yourself," I growled.

"Are all you girls enjoying your holiday?" Mrs. Gilpin said, and we all chorused, "Oo-oo-h, yes!"

She went on, "Let me compliment you on your appearance. Mrs. Folds, you've turned them out extremely well, and I wish them the best of luck but I hope they'll let our locals win *something*."

116

"Not to worry, they'll probably win everything," mumbled Billie Smith in my left ear, and we both tried to stifle our giggles.

The rest of the time passed quickly, and by the time we were all dressed and the ponies were ready to the last smooth hair, other competitors were arriving and the scene began to look lively. There were about thirty competitors including ourselves, in different age groups, and while the small children's class was doing its stuff Ann and I discovered a table full of prizes and hopefully decided what we should like to have if we were lucky enough to win anything.

I said, "If I win those stirrup irons, will you give me a pound for them, and then I can buy some emerald wool for Mummy to knit me a sweater like Mrs. Gilpin's?" and Ann said, "Are you kidding?"

At last it was time for the under-sixteens to be called into the ring, and all of a sudden I got that glorious feeling you sometimes get when the sun is shining and the turf is bright green and the white rails are beckoning and the judge looks deceptively benevolent and the ponies are prancing and you're dying to be off at the jumps.

I don't say that this is always the right feeling to have, it can be jolly dangerous, that is if you let yourself get topped up and careless and think, nothing can happen to me today because I'm the Queen of the May, and that sort of bonkers idea. Then you find yourself riding out of the ring with twelve faults, and you blame it on bad luck or on anything else but yourself.

So when I got the aforesaid feeling I thought, "Beware, Beware!" like the maiden in the Awful Avalanche poem.

We led the ponies round to inspect the jumps.

"Tell me if I'm wrong," said Wendy, "but I'd say whoever planned this course wasn't with it. The actual jumps aren't bad, but it's the pacing. It's enough to give a pony hiccups in its hoofs."

"Oh, I'd say it was just a bit sporting," said Jackie.

"Sporting! You try the distance between the wall and the gate. You'll have to practically come to a dead stop before your take-off. I noticed the juniors nearly all got four faults at the gate and now I know why."

"So if everybody gets four faults at the gate we'll be all equal, won't we?" said Mercy naïvely.

"But that's not all," said Ann. "We have to do an in-and-out which the kids hadn't, and there isn't even room for one proper pace in the middle. What do they think we're riding—leopards, or something?"

"Oh, come on," I said. "Let's ride the course. No good beefing about it."

Ann had the bad luck to have to ride first. She took the first three jumps beautifully, but as she approached the wall I could see she was worrying about that pacing so I wasn't surprised when she got four faults there and four more at the gate. She then pulled herself together and did a jaunty cat jump at the in-and-out.

Everybody followed the same pattern, eight faults, twelve faults. It was monotonous.

"Oh, dear, isn't anybody going to do a clear round?" said Mrs. Gilpin plaintively.

It was more than we could bear, and Diana said rashly, "Not on that course. It's murder. It must have been paced out by a blind grasshopper—if it was ever paced out at all."

There was a deathly hush and Mrs. Gilpin went a sort of pale mauve. We then realised that she must have constructed the course herself, without reference to experts. Diana didn't know which way to look, and unfortunately she was just due to ride, so what with embarrassment and everything else she got fourteen faults.

I was drawn to ride last but one. Strangely enough, the best up to then was our fat little April who went for the jumps as if she was in a circus and couldn't care less what happened, bouncing about on her pony, hopping and curvetting and doing all the wrong things while Mrs. Folds kept wincing and saying, "Oh, isn't she awful!" But she ended up with only four faults, and got those at the easiest jump of the lot.

Rosevale Washington rode just before me, with a big grin on her face. She also behaved circus-wise, and she happened to have a pony who could double himself up like a jack-knife. In addition to this she was a fearless, dashing sort of rider and as cool as a lollipop. She treated the course as one big joke, and had everybody laughing.

"It's fun to watch, and in this case it seems to have brought home the bacon," said Mrs. Folds as Rosevale, standing up in her stirrups and patting her pony's neck, rode in amid thunderous applause with the first clear round. "But nobody could describe it as equitation in the classic sense."

"Oh, gosh!" said Wendy. "As if anybody could equitate classically on that course. Pierrot got his legs twisted like corkscrews before he'd done."

"Now it's you, Jill," said Mrs. Folds. "Jolly good luck. And just for the honour of the troop, try not to look like something out of a Wild West film."

"I'll try," I said, "but the only way to go at that course is like a trick jumper. The poor local Pony

Club people have done worse than we have. They look awfully cheesed off."

I rode as well as I could and I had all the luck in the world. Twice Black Boy's hoofs made contact with a rattle that seemed to shake the rails, but nothing fell. At the difficult bits I kept him right up to the bridle, and managed to hit him exactly on the take-off stride, and though he gave a few muffled snorts of indignation he jumped like an angel, and we pulled it off. Clear round!

"We've done it," said Rosevale slapping me on the back as I dismounted. "Rah, rah, the trekkers!"

"What happens now?" piped Billie Smith. "Do Jill and Rosevale jump it off?"

"Not if I can help it," I said, fanning myself dramatically, and Rosevale chimed in, "Not for a thousand dollars. I'd get forty faults."

Mrs. Gilpin came up and asked us what we wanted to do, and we said we'd decided to share the first place. Third was a boy from the local Pony Club who had only two faults, and April was fourth, and swaggering around as if she'd won a gold cup at Richmond.

Rosevale and I each got a Boots Gift Token for £2, and Rosevale offered to buy mine for 25/-, so I took it and made sure of that emerald wool.

"Now let's have the jumps cleared away," said Mrs. Gilpin, "and join in some jolly games." So we all plunged gaily into Musical Sacks, Egg and Spoon races, and team games, and not only did most people manage to win prizes but Mrs. Gilpin gave a small prize to every competitor just for entering, which was jolly generous of her, and even Mercy had three prizes to take home to show her aunt.

Mrs. Gilpin then led the way to a vast coach house

121

where long tables were set out with a magnificent tea.

"I'm sorry about the course," she said, blushing. "I'm afraid it put some people off."

"Let's forget about the course," said Mrs. Folds. "Nobody came to any harm and I think everybody will admit they've had the time of their lives."

We all shouted hurray! and Wendy said, "Three cheers for Mrs. Gilpin!" and we nearly took the roof off.

The local newspaper photographer came in and took flashes of the long tables and the feast and everybody holding up their prizes, and Ann said, "I call this a smashing end to the pony trek."

The Glorious End

AFTER tea all the guests departed, and we helped with the massive task of clearing everything up, which took all the evening.

At last we relaxed outside our tents in the beautiful summer evening and everybody was full of happiness.

"I've enjoyed today the best of all," said Katy Smith. "I won the Bending race, too. Oh, why do you always begin to enjoy yourself the most just when it's time to go home? To think, this time to-morrow we'll all be at home and it'll all be over!"

"It only seems about two days since we started off," said Wendy. "I wish it was beginning instead of ending."

We all chorused, "Don't we all!"

"When you come to look back on it," said Ann, "nothing much has actually happened. I mean, not the sort of things that happen in books, like buried treasure and getting drowned, but it's been such *fun*."

"Daddy told me before I started that I'd wreck the trek," said April, "and I haven't."

"Not for want of trying," yelled Rosevale, and April made a dive at her and sent all the coffee beakers flying—fortunately they were empty—and everybody started singing Don't Wreck the Trek to the tune of "Don't Knock the Rock."

By now a bright pink sunset was dying away behind the trees, and when we had rescued the beakers we made coffee on a primus stove and helped ourselves to the big basket of buns and cakes which Mrs.

Gilpin had sent down, and had a bit of a singsong, and then we all faded away into our tents and were soon fast asleep because we had to make an early start tomorrow.

While the cooks were getting our six o'clock breakfast in the hush of the morning dew, so to speak, Billie Smith was finishing off her Poetical Account of the Trek.

She showed me the last bit. It said:

"The last morning comes all too soon
And we shall be home this afternoon,
Good-bye to all the fun and pleasure,
When we get home we shall have too much
    leisure,
We shall remember each lovely ride,
With lots of sad regrets and pride,
And all the smashing food we had,
The pains of parting will be bad."

"It's jolly good," I said. "Sort of sad and beautiful."

"Let's have a look," said Ann. She turned back a few pages and read aloud:

"We are sitting in a shady nook,
Waiting for the sausages to cook,
The birds are singing up above,
This is the sort of life I love."

"It isn't really very good," said Billie modestly, "but when I get home I'll copy it out, and then when I read it over I can remember everything."

"I like that bit about, 'This is the kind of life I love'," I said, "because it's so jolly true."

"Pony helpers forward!" shouted Mrs. Folds. "The vans will be here in an hour. Everything packed?"

April said, "Isn't it funny, everything goes in your saddle-bags when you start, and when you come home there's the same stuff and only half of it goes in. It sort of swells, I suppose."

We ate our breakfast of piping hot sausages, and everybody was sadly thinking. "This is the last time."

I said to Ann, "I vote for the rest of the holidays we have breakfast in our orchard at six o'clock, and you come round and Diana and Wendy."

"It wouldn't be the same without all the others," said Ann.

Then the vans arrived and the ponies were led in to go to the train, and a coach came for us to take us to the station, about an hour later.

"I've arranged for the ponies to be taken off at the station before Chatton," said Mrs. Folds. "I thought it would be fun to ride the last few miles and arrive home looking like a returning pony trek."

We all brightened up as we thought this was a marvellous idea.

Mrs. Gilpin came down from the house and shook hands with us all, and said how sorry she was to see us go.

"You must come again," she said, and we all said that was the one thing we'd love to do.

"Won't it feel grue sitting in a coach?" said Diana. "A sort of anti-climax, and frightfully tame."

But it didn't turn out quite so tame as all that, because the first thing the coach did was to take us to the wrong station, which was on the wrong line, and we didn't discover that until we were all on the platform and Mrs. Folds had gone to buy the tickets, and the coach had gone away.

Panic and chaos. Mrs. Folds rushed off to telephone the place where the coach came from to tell them to send it back for us when it arrived there.

"Now we're going to lose our train," she said, "and

the ponies will be waiting for us at Felton and there'll be nobody there to cope with them."

"Couldn't we send a telegram to Felton to send the ponies back again?" said April hopefully. "And then we could have a few more days at Mrs. Gilpin's."

But actually at that moment the coach returned, as the driver had suddenly discovered his mistake and had turned back for us, so we piled in, and had just driven away when Mercy discovered that she had left her purse on a seat at the station.

So back we had to go, and Mrs. Folds looked cross, and some people looked worried, but most of us were giggling and couldn't have cared less by then because it was getting to be really funny.

Mercy began to weep, and Billie Smith said, "I wrote The End on my poem after breakfast, and now I'll have to scratch it out and write quite a lot more."

Everybody shouted, "We'll do it for you," and started suggesting lines.

At last we got to the proper station and with just one minute to spare before the train arrived. We tumbled out of the coach and thundered into the station, and of course discovered that we had to cross the bridge. We raced across like hares and saw the train coming in as we clattered down the steps. Somebody tore open a door and we all bundled into the corridor of the train and gradually found seats.

"Don't tell me everybody's here!" said Mrs. Folds, walking round with her tie under one ear. "That would be too much to expect. I've got a feeling that April is still on the coach and Mercy tying her shoe up on the bridge."

"I've counted up and they're all correct," said Wendy. "*There's* April—she actually found time to get a chocolate bar out of the slot machine—and Mercy's having hysterics in the next carriage."

"Thank goodness," said Mrs. Folds. "Now everybody can take turns to tidy up, and we'll all disembark at Felton looking as if nothing has happened. April, if you have chocolate on your face at Felton you don't ride to Chatton with us. Understood?"

We each had a packet of sandwiches which Mrs. Gilpin had prepared for us—she really was a wonderful person who thought of everything—and at half-past one we arrived at Felton and climbed down from the train. Mrs. Folds inspected us.

"The shirts might be cleaner," she said, "but I suppose that's too much to expect at the end of a trek. Everybody's hair right? Good."

The ponies were ready for us, and we mounted and rode off in double file towards Chatton, along the grass verges of the familiar lanes.

And just before we got to Chatton village, when we thought it was all going to fade away into nothingness, Ann suddenly said, "What's that?"

Right across the lane was a banner on poles. It was made of bright yellow cotton, and stitched on it in scarlet letters were the words, "WELCOME HOME, TREKKERS."

Underneath the banner were quite a lot of people, who turned out to be mothers and brothers and sisters, and they were all waving to us. And right in front stood Miss Crombie, grinning like the rising sun, and holding a big basket.

She came to meet us.

"Welcome to the pony trekkers!" she said. "Jolly well done!" And out of her basket she took a posy for every one of us, and started fastening them on the ponies' browbands.

"I say, this is rather grand!" said Mrs. Folds. "What a wonderful idea."

"I'm so glad you like it," said Miss Crombie, and added modestly, "I thought of it myself, and I made the banner."

Everybody's relations came flocking round, including Mummy, and said, "Have you had a good time?" and we all said, "Absolutely smashing."

Miss Crombie came up to me.

"I don't know how to thank you for your postcard," she said. "It was so jolly kind of you to think of me. You've no idea how it cheered me up." Which shows that if you do little things for people it always seems to mean a lot to them.

"I vote we break up the party here," said Mrs. Folds. "It's been such a magnificent welcome that anything else would be a come-down. So let's all say au revoir to each other."

"Before you break up," said Miss Crombie, "there's just one think I'd like to tell you. While you've been away I've bought a small field which I'd like to present to the Pony Club, and I thought I'd fit it up with some jumps so that you can practise during the winter."

We all gasped. It was a dream come true.

"Gosh!" said Wendy. "It feels like Christmas Day! Three cheers for Miss Crombie."

Everybody started cheering, the whole of Chatton must have wondered what was going on, and when the noise had died down I said, "And three more cheers for Mrs. Folds for taking us on that gorgeous trek!"

And again we woke the echoes.

What a thrilling end to the pony trek!